The Lake House

SOUTHERN CHARM
BOOK TWO

LILLY MIRREN

Chapter One

Julie Brown stared at the laptop screen and blinked. She couldn't focus, and that wasn't like her. She'd studied for years to get into the Psychology PhD program at the University of Georgia. It was her dream. At least, it had been until two months ago. In June, she'd learned a secret about her family that had turned her life upside down. On the outside, she was still living the same way she had been. But on the inside, everything was different. It was as though she didn't know herself any longer. Who was she? Where was she from? All these questions buzzed around inside her, and even though she now knew the answers, it didn't quiet the discontent that had crept in and taken residence in her innermost parts.

With a sigh, she slammed the laptop shut and walked out the door, careful to push her dorm room key into her shorts pocket. Then she skipped down the stairs to the foyer. There were rows of mailboxes set into the far wall. She hurried over to them and dug her mailbox key out of her pocket. It shared a key ring with the dorm key. They both dangled next to her car keys against a backdrop of Betty Boop. It was something her mother had given her years earlier and she'd never had the heart to get rid of it, even if it didn't suit her personality or style. It meant the world to her. After her mother died, everything related to her meant the world to Julie. She couldn't cling on to it hard enough, or hold fast enough, or remember clearly enough—that time in her life was a blur of loss, pain, sorrow and anger.

She caught sight of her reflection in the silver surface of the mailboxes. Her long brown hair was parted in the middle and her black-rimmed glasses made her look earnest. She pushed her hair behind her shoulders and reached for the mail.

There were a few flyers and an envelope with the university seal on it, no doubt her latest fees statement. She was closing the mailbox door again when a familiar voice spoke up.

"Hey, Julie. Haven't seen you lately."

Her ex-boyfriend, Zane, lounged against the mailboxes and casually crossed one foot over the other with a lazy smile. "How've ya been?"

Zane lived in the building. It was how they met. But so far she'd managed to avoid running into him too often since their break up. She did her best to smile back. "Hi, Zane. I'm well. And you?"

"Pretty good. You weren't at the party last night. It was off the hook."

Julie knew it was *off the hook*—she'd heard it from a block away. "Sounds like you had a great time. I was a bit tired." That, plus she was twenty-five years old, soon to be twenty-six. *Off-the-hook* parties were not really on her list of priorities these days. That's what she got for dating a man four years younger than herself. "You're a senior now. Planning on studying anytime soon?"

He laughed. "You haven't changed."

"No, I haven't."

"How's your PhD coming?"

"It's okay. I'm stuck right now. Finding it hard to focus,

what with all the parties going on. I'm planning on moving out of the dorms and finding an apartment somewhere in Athens as soon as I can locate one in my price range." Julie flipped through her mail.

"That makes sense, I guess. Why don't you just take some time off?"

"I couldn't do that."

"Well, it's somethin' to think about. See you around," he said, waving goodbye.

As she walked slowly back up the stairs to her dorm room, Julie realised to her surprise that Zane had a point. In theory, she could take time off. There was no reason why not. She'd never actually done it before, had always been focused on getting through her studies as quickly as she could manage. She was a good student — always the first to class, always had her assignments done on time. She'd never considered taking a break from her studies. But, there was a first time for everything.

It was strange to see him. They'd broken up about six months ago, and at the time she'd been heartbroken. In a way. It wasn't that she'd loved him, but she'd loved who she was through his eyes. The way he adored her. And he was so handsome, cool and fun. She'd never thought a man like that would be interested in her. But he had been. And he'd wanted to keep things going, but he wasn't ready for anything serious.

He liked to go to parties and to pull pranks on his frat buddies. His idea of a good time was to drink beer at the *Mellow Mushroom* pizza parlour until he was blind drunk. Then he and his friends would run through the streets of Athens daring each other to do stupid things while she trailed behind, hoping they didn't get hurt and wondering how on earth she got there. When it was the two of them alone, he was thoughtful, kind and intelligent. But so much of his life revolved around his fraternity that those times became more and more rare until finally, she couldn't do it any longer.

The breakup seemed like a decade ago now. After all she'd been through since then—all the tumult, the revelations about her family, Aunt Rita's illness—she felt as though she'd been through the wringer and had struggled to sleep soundly most nights. That now showed up as dark smudges beneath her eyes and a haggard kind of look that scared her when she glanced in the mirror, so mostly she tried to avoid anything that showed her reflection these days. Instead, she chose to hurry through life, lost in thought, hoping that soon she'd manage to get some words written for her thesis, or perhaps a full night of sleep that evening.

She *could* take time off. Why hadn't she thought of that before? She'd always been so invested in her future. Everything in her life had been geared towards this—her potential career. Could she step aside? Even as the thought filtered through her mind, she knew she had to do it. She was burned out. Had nothing left to give. She'd take some time off. Her supervisor wouldn't mind—she knew what Julie had been going through.

Back in the dorm room, she quickly packed up the rest of her things. She'd already begun packing boxes the previous week, determined to move into an apartment as soon as she could find an affordable one. She'd call the movers and have them take her things to storage, and then she'd go home. She sighed, relief washing over her. It was time. She was ready. The only thing she could think to do now was to spend some time at the lake house with Aunt Rita.

* * *

On the drive home, Julie listened to music and tried to relax. It'd been three days since she made the decision to leave the

University of Georgia campus, and she'd spent that time frantically packing the remainder of her things, giving notice to the RA in her dormitory, talking with her supervisor about a hiatus on her studies, and spreading the word throughout her acquaintances.

It didn't take her long to realise she'd failed to make any decent friendships during her time there. Most of the undergrads she'd socialised with had moved away right after graduation and she'd lost contact with them, and the post-grad students kept mostly to themselves. It was depressing to admit she hadn't had a decent friendship since senior year three years ago. She'd kept so busy with her studies, boyfriends or dates that she hadn't thought much about it. Now that she was single again, she suddenly saw with new clarity how lonely she was.

She didn't have time to stop in at the lake house. Aunt Rita had called the previous night to ask if she'd pick her up from Piedmont Hospital after a chemotherapy treatment, so that's where she headed first.

The Piedmont Cancer Institute had become familiar to her in recent weeks, since she'd accompanied Aunt Rita there a few times. She hurried through the carpeted waiting area and found her aunt in one of the treatment rooms, still receiving chemotherapy.

Rita looked wiped out. Her face was pale, and she lay back on the recliner with her eyes shut. Julie bent to kiss her forehead and grasped her hand to squeeze it. Aunt Rita's eyes flew open, and she smiled wide.

"There you are, honey. I thought you'd be gettin' here soon. I've missed you." She reached up to pinch Julie's cheeks.

Julie laughed. "Ouch. You always do that."

"And I always will." Aunt Rita grinned, a little colour returning to her face. "You have the most pinchable cheeks. Have ever since the day you were born."

"Do you think I have time to go to the restroom?" Julie asked.

Aunt Rita glanced at her watch. "I'll be here for at least another half hour."

"Do you mind if I go now? I've been fit to burst for about an hour."

"You go on, honey. I'll be here waiting."

Julie bustled down the hallway in search of a restroom. She found one and did her business, then ducked out into the hall again and stood looking right and left for a few seconds. The hallway was nondescript, with automatic glass doors whichever way she went. She spun to face the restroom, then tried to remember which way she'd turned to get there. Hmmm... left, perhaps. So that meant she should leave by turning right. She should've paid more attention, but she was so focused on relieving her screaming bladder that she hadn't taken in her surroundings.

She strode towards the doors. They flew open, and she walked into a waiting room decorated in muted blues and reds. No, this definitely wasn't right. She didn't remember anything that looked like this. She spun on her heel to go back in the other direction and collided with a man in a white coat. His stethoscope knocked her in the nose.

"Whoops! I'm so sorry." She took a step back as he reached for her shoulders with both hands to steady her.

"Are you okay?" His deep voice sounded kind and soothing.

She looked up to smile in apology and then gaped. "Jamie?"

She recognised him immediately. She'd known him when she was a child. He'd stayed with her and her mother for almost a year when his parents were going through a divorce. He was fifteen at the time, and she was twelve. He'd been like a brother to her, but they'd lost contact when he moved back in with his mother at her new place in Gulf Shores, Alabama. It'd been over a decade since she'd seen him.

He studied her with a half smile on his face. He didn't recognise her, she could tell, but he was scrambling to figure out who she was. She'd changed a lot from the shy twelve-year-old girl he'd known.

"I go by James now... good to see you again..."

"Julie Brown..." she reminded him.

His blue eyes widened. "Julie? Wow. You've grown up. It's been a long time."

"You work here?"

He nodded. "That's right. I've been at this hospital for about twelve months. I like it here. And what about you? Are you still living in the area?"

"I was at UGA but I'm home again now, staying with Aunt Rita for a while."

"That's great. Listen, I've got to keep moving. Patients to see. But I'm glad we ran into each other. I hope I see you again."

She waved goodbye and watched him walk away. He looked handsome in his scrubs and white coat. His sandy blond hair was a little mussed where he'd no doubt run his fingers through it, and he walked with an air of confidence and urgency. He strode along the hall and then disappeared through a doorway. She stayed where she was, feeling a little shaken.

The last time she'd seen him, she was with her mother. They'd stood in the front yard, waving goodbye as he drove away. He'd turned at the last minute to look out through the passenger window and raised a hand, his gaze fixing on Julie. He'd seemed sad to be leaving, although she knew he was excited to be back with his mother again, even if her life was weighed down by chaos and conflict.

With a sigh, Julie continued on her way and found Rita

again without too much trouble. The halls all looked the same, but it didn't take her long to finally spot a vending machine she'd passed by earlier.

"There you are," Rita said. "I was beginning to think I'd have to send out a search party."

Julie laughed. "I'm here. No need for a search party."

Chapter Two

What was I thinking?

The words drifted through Rita Osbourne's mind for the hundredth time in a month. She'd invited her cousin, Cathy, to help run the Honeysuckle Café with her, and so far it was going about as badly as anyone could've imagined. Especially in light of the fact that Cathy had previously threatened legal action over the cafe ownership. Rita had no desire to spend her days in a courtroom or to pay a lawyer her hard-earned money. It seemed easier to mend fences and hope for the best. Thankfully, Cathy had backed down on that front, but it still left a stench in the air between them. And besides that, Cathy was bossy, overbearing, rude and about a thousand other unpleasant things that Rita really could do without considering she was currently suffering under the effects of chemotherapy.

She sat in her office, listening to Cathy rant on and on about the staff.

"Would you shut the door behind you, please?" She tried to keep her tone upbeat, but it was difficult. What she really wanted was a nap. A nice, long afternoon nap.

Cathy huffed, shut the door, then stood with her arms folded over her chest. "You can't just ignore things and hope they'll go away, Rita."

Rita scratched her head and leaned back in her chair. "I know that, Cathy. I'm listenin'."

Cathy wore an aqua jogging suit with a large purple slash across the front of the jacket and pants. There was a matching purple headband pulled tight around her blonde locks, although her hair was a little more grey than blonde these days, and her heavily made-up blue eyes flashed. She looked as though she'd stepped out of a time machine from the eighties. It'd been her favourite decade, and she made certain everyone remembered it whenever they looked at her.

"When Chuck came in this morning, he didn't lock the door behind him. I know this because I came in after him and it was unlocked. Anyone could enter the premises at that time. And with only one or two staff on duty, it could cause problems. The café should be locked until it's time to open."

"I agree—I'll have a word with Chuck. He has a lot on his mind in the morning."

"He's a cook, not a rocket scientist."

Wow. "Okay, Cathy, thanks for that. I appreciate you lookin' into these things and helping make the café run more smoothly."

Cathy opened the door. "You're too soft on the staff, Rita. They run roughshod all over you."

Rita arched an eyebrow. "I'll take that on board."

The door slammed shut, and Rita sighed with relief. Alone at last. She pressed both hands to her face and stifled a yawn that threatened to split her face in two. Matilda, her newly discovered niece from Australia, had asked her why she continued to put up with Cathy's presence at the café during their last shift together, but it was difficult for her to understand, let alone explain. She felt she owed it to her cousin. After all, Cathy had a point: both their fathers had started the place.

There was a connection for each of them. And usually Rita might have ignored Cathy's demands, but with her cancer treatment underway, she needed all the help she could get. Matilda had been fantastic since she came over from Australia, but she was young, newly married and a vet on hiatus. Rita wasn't naïve enough to believe she'd stick around forever. And her niece, Julie, was going to be a psychologist. Rita needed a backup plan. And unfortunately, Cathy was it.

She was determined to train Cathy. It was proving harder than she'd thought it would be, but surely her cousin had to take some of the lessons she taught her on board eventually. She only hoped the café would survive it. If the staff stuck around during the training period, she'd be pleasantly surprised. She'd have to remember to buy them each some thank-you chocolates when she was next at the store.

While answering a few emails, Rita thought about Cathy and what she could do to help her cousin feel more connected to the café. She didn't want her to be so anxious all the time, worrying about every little thing, but to relax, learn to love the place and the people who worked there. Rita adored the café. She loved Chuck the cook and Amanda the manager as well as all the wait and kitchen staff who came and went based on their casual schedules and needs. It was always buzzing with activities, laughter and fun. Usually, she'd be right in the middle of it all, but now, she didn't have the energy. And she needed Cathy to keep her finger on the pulse of the place without upsetting everyone there.

She shuffled across the floor of the cramped office space to the large metal cabinets in the back. Opening both doors, she scanned the contents. There were some old photos in there somewhere. She recalled seeing them once but couldn't quite remember where they were. Then she spotted it—a metal box. It wasn't locked. She pulled it out of the cabinet and set it on her desk, then sat again with a deep exhale of air. Everything ached. It felt good to sit down.

Inside the box, there was a stack of photographs. Old photos of the café. The staff, her father, Uncle Bill, her kids Tyler and Sophie when they were little, and even her sister Helen with little Julie. By the time she'd flipped through all of the photographs, there were tears on her cheeks, and her heart ached along with the rest of her body.

An idea came to her—what if she printed some new copies of a few of these photographs, framed them and hung them around the café? It would make for some great nostalgic ambiance, and it might help Cathy better connect with the place and stop acting so high-strung. She'd been an anxious kid, quick to judge and critique others, but she'd only gotten worse in her older years. It was as though she was a piece of twine that'd been stretched tighter and tighter with every year of her life, and right now, she was ready to snap. Rita didn't know what to do to help break the tension without snapping the string, but she hoped these photographs might start the process.

If she remembered rightly, there was some other memorabilia at the lake house. A few albums, trinkets and so on, locked away in a closet that she never accessed. It'd been her dad's closet when she was a kid. After he died, she didn't have the heart to go through it. Just the thought of throwing any of his things away made her squirm, and looking through it might put her in a puddle of tears. But the way she was feeling right now, things couldn't get much more emotional. With everything she was going through due to her cancer diagnosis, the news that Matilda had brought with her from Australia

about her family, the struggles she'd been having at the café …
surely some old photos and junk from the past wouldn't make
her feel any worse. It might even cheer her up to see some of
Dad's old things now that the sting of his passing had faded.

Chapter Three

Julie waded through a murky cloud. It seemed strange that there were clouds around her feet, but not so strange that she should question it. So, she walked forwards, hands outstretched, thrashing them about as if to move the clouds away. But the clouds wouldn't budge. They simply floated around her hands, like the little fish she used to try to catch when she paddled on the edges of Jackson Lake.

When she blinked, she found that she was actually in her house. Back at home with Mom. She could hear her mother downstairs in the kitchen, clanking around making supper. She hoped it would involve biscuits or hoecakes. Anything with biscuits or hoecakes was just fine with her. As long as there was a tonne of butter and strawberry jelly to go with them, or maybe some buttermilk.

Mom called her name from the kitchen. Julie traipsed happily down the stairs. When she saw her mother standing at the counter, with flour on her hands and a little dab on the end of her nose, a rush of joy and pain swept over her. She leapt at her mother with a little cry and buried her face in

Mom's shoulder, grasping onto the floral apron tied neatly around her neck and trim waist.

Mom stroked her hair, laughing. "What's gotten into you?"

Julie couldn't answer. She didn't know what had gotten into her, only that she was so happy to see her mother and wouldn't ever let go of her again. She *couldn't* let go of her. She had to hold on tight. She looked up at her mother's smiling face and felt another wave of joy that brought tears to her eyes.

Mom always had the prettiest smile, with her long blonde hair and her sparkling blue eyes. Julie wished she looked like her mother. Everyone always complimented Mom, saying she was beautiful. That she could've done anything with her life. But Mom said she didn't care about any of that—all she wanted to do with her life was to have Julie. To raise her, spend every day kissing and tickling her, and making biscuits with strawberry jelly for her to eat. Julie loved it when she talked like that, although she realised in the moment she was probably a little too old to still be burying her head in her mother. But she hadn't had her growth spurt yet, and her head only reached as far as her mom's shoulder. She wondered if she'd ever be as tall.

"I called you downstairs because there's something I want to talk to you about." Mom pulled a barstool out from the counter and patted the top of it.

Julie climbed onto the stool, crossed her ankles and waited.

Mom sighed. "A friend of mine is going through a hard time. She's getting a divorce, and there's a lot going on that I can't really tell you. The upshot is that she's asked if we'll let her boy stay with us a while."

Julie frowned. "Huh?"

"I don't know if you remember James Fuller... Jamie is probably what you called him."

"Jamie? No."

Mom dipped her head. "Never mind. He's a little older than you. Three years, I think. But I said he could stay here. He's a nice boy. He attends the local high school and he's on the baseball team, so you probably won't see too much of him."

"Oh, okay."

"You don't mind?" Mom's brow furrowed, as though she was worried what Julie might say.

"I guess not." Although Julie couldn't imagine having a boy live with them. She'd never lived with a boy, or a man. Her father had died before she was born. And even though she'd stayed at the lake house with her grandparents on occasion, it was always a short-term thing. "How long will he be here?"

Mom's lips pursed while she thought. "I don't know. A few months. Maybe six?"

"Six months?" Julie exclaimed, her eyes wide. "I thought you meant he'd stay for the weekend or something."

Mom laughed awkwardly. "No, a bit longer than that. His parents have to work some things out, and his mother is moving to Alabama. She didn't want to pull him out partway through the school year."

"When will he arrive?"

"Any minute now."

Julie realised then it was a done deal. It didn't much matter what she had to say about it. She didn't want a strange boy to come live in their home. But it was clear Mom didn't want to hear it. So instead, she offered a wan smile and went to the formal dining room to sit by the bay windows and look out at the driveway. If he was coming, she'd see him from there and could decide whether or not she liked him.

She watched a procession of ants on the windowsill when she got bored. They traipsed in single file over the white timber, dodging around one of their pals who'd stopped still for some inexplicable reason. On her knees, forehead pressed to the glass, she studied their little ant bodies, their antennae moving as though searching for something, and the hurried pace they never gave up.

Finally, a car pulled into the driveway. It was more of a minivan, really. Julie was glad her mother didn't drive a minivan. They had a sedan. It was much less embarrassing at the middle school drop-off. Although, if she could've had brothers and sisters to fill the seats of a minivan, she'd have been willing to put up with the embarrassment. She'd always wanted siblings, but it was never going to happen. Mom said she needed to get over that and be grateful for what she had. To count her blessings, since no one knew how many days on this earth God granted us.

She was talking about Dad. Julie knew that. Her mother still cried sometimes. At night when it was quiet, Julie could hear her. Julie cried too, but for a different reason. She cried because she'd never know her father. And because she desperately longed to be part of a normal family with a father, mother, sisters or brothers. But it was selfish of her to keep pining over something Mom could do nothing about. So, she kept it to herself.

A boy climbed out of the passenger side of the minivan. A woman stepped out of the driver's side. Mom met the woman with a hug, and they spoke quietly together for a few minutes while the boy stood in silence, a roller bag by his feet, and a jacket hanging over one arm.

Then the woman gave him a hug and drove away. He watched the van disappear around the bend at the end of the street. His sandy blond hair was mussed and pointed in every direction. His eyes squinted after the van. His lightly freckled nose was wrinkled.

Mom said something to him, and he followed her to the front door. Julie's heart skipped a beat. They were coming inside. She hurried over to the piano and began plonking out a tune on the keys, doing her best to pretend she'd been busy this whole time and hadn't had her face plastered to the bay window to watch him arrive.

She waited until he'd settled his things in his room and wandered back downstairs before she said more than hi. She followed him into the kitchen then poured herself a glass of ice-cold lemonade.

"You want one?" she asked.

He nodded. "Thanks."

She poured another glass and slid it across the counter to him, then sipped on hers. It was tangy and sweet, just the way she liked it. She and Mom had made it with lemons from their tree yesterday.

"It's good," he said.

"Do people call you James?"

"Jamie," he replied without expression.

"Okay. Everyone just calls me Julie... so you can call me that. If you want." Her stomach dropped. She wasn't sure she'd ever said something so idiotic before. She willed herself to simply stop talking.

His eyes narrowed. "Okay. Super."

"I can show you the lake..." she offered.

He glanced out the glass windows that looked over the water. "That one?"

Her cheeks flamed. "Uh, yeah."

"Sure. Why not?"

With a sigh of relief, she walked out through the side door onto the deck. "Lake Jackson... there's good fishin'."

She wasn't sure what else to say. The lake was fairly self-evident. The water was dark. There were houses nestled amongst the trees all around its scalloped edges, and a few ducks flew low across the water.

"Okay... catfish?"

"Yep. And bass, too."

"Cool."

"Do you fish?"

"I've never done it," he replied. "But I wouldn't mind givin' it a try sometime."

His blond hair flopped over his eyes, and he blew it back with a puff of air.

"I'll take you out on the boat."

"Okay. Thanks."

"How old are you?"

"Fifteen. You?"

"I'm twelve. I'll be thirteen next month."

He reached out a hand and grabbed her by the arm, shaking it. Then Julie's eyes blinked open, and she found herself in bed with a dog licking her cheek.

"Ugh. Blue, stop it." She pushed the dog away. He came at her again, tail wagging. Blue loved this game. His long tongue found her nose.

She sneezed and he backed up, tail still wagging. She flung her legs over the side of the bed and leaned over her knees with a yawn. It was still dark out. She padded down the hall with Blue close behind, his tongue lolling.

Outside, the night air was cool. She'd forgotten her glasses, so everything was a little out of focus. She should've thrown on a sweater as well but hadn't thought of it. Instead, she hugged herself and stood looking up at the moon where it hung above the tree line. She sat down on one of the Adirondack chairs on the deck and sighed. Her throat tightened.

The vision of her mother in the dream had made her entire body ache with the sorrow of losing her. It was as if she'd had a chance to travel back in time and see her again, but the realisation that the woman she'd called Mom until the day she died wasn't her biological mother hit her like a mallet to the gut. When Matilda came to Georgia, she had disrupted all their lives. But what no one else seemed to care about was the fact that Julie's entire identity had been wrapped up in her mother. And now that was gone.

The only person who'd truly loved her was gone. She'd never met her biological parents—hadn't known a father at all. Tears poured down her cheeks, and deep sobs erupted from her throat. It was too much to bear. Who was she? Where did she belong? And why had this part of herself been stolen away when she'd already lost so much?

Chapter Four

Rita woke up the next morning feeling a little better. She rolled out of bed, and after a quick shower, she tugged on a floral dress, then wandered out to the kitchen to make breakfast. She didn't intend to go into the café this morning. Cathy and Matilda had it all under control. She needed the rest and she'd managed to sleep late, which was a pleasant change from her normal routine.

She began by mixing cornmeal pancake batter using a Jiffy box. Then she scrambled some eggs and cooked grits with butter and cream on the stove. Just as she was finishing up, Julie stumbled into the kitchen, rubbing bleary eyes.

Rita laughed. "Hey there, sleepyhead."

Julie yawned and sat on a barstool. "What time is it?"

"Ten o'clock."

"Wow. I can't believe I fell back to sleep. I was up half the night."

"Why? What's going on?"

Julie sighed. "I was thinking about Mom."

Rita nodded. She understood. Her sister Helen had died about a decade ago from an undiagnosed heart condition when Julie was still too young to lose a mother. Julie had been a lost, scared and angry fifteen-year-old when she stood by her mother's grave, all dressed in black and with red-rimmed eyes. Rita would never forget it. Her heart had broken that day.

"I know she'd want to be here with you, honey. She loved you so much."

Julie's eyes filled with tears. They looked hollowed out, as though she'd been crying.

"I can't help wondering if she knew about Matilda."

Rita had thought the same thing many times. "It's no good to worry about it. We'll never understand exactly what she knew or didn't know. Or how she felt about it. If she knew, she chose to keep you. Do you realise that?"

Julie's brow furrowed. "I guess I didn't think of it that way."

"Honey, if she knew Matilda was her blood-related child, she chose to keep and raise you rather than get Matilda back. That has to stand for somethin'."

Julie's face crumpled, and tears spilled onto her cheeks. "You're right. It does mean somethin' to me. Thank you."

Rita waddled around the counter to hug her niece. "I know you're dealing with a lot, sweetheart. But you'll get through this. We both will."

Rita dished them each a plate of breakfast, then they sat at the small round kitchen table to eat. Rita said grace, and they dug in.

The pancakes were soft and fluffy. The syrup sweetened the salty grits and eggs, and the whole thing together was exactly what Rita needed. She let her eyes drift shut as she chewed a mouthful. "My favourite — corn pancakes. The syrup just sinks right on in."

"They're delicious," Julie agreed. "How are you feelin' today?"

"Not too bad. Which of course means I've got chemo tomorrow."

"Do you want me to drive you?" Julie asked.

"That would be great, honey. I appreciate it. It's my last treatment for a little while. They want to give my body some time to recover before I go again."

"You're so strong, Auntie Rita. I'm really impressed by how well you're managin' all of this. It's a lot."

Rita smiled. "Thanks, honey. Have I told you how happy I am that you're here?"

"Only a few times," Julie replied with a grin.

"Well, that's because I mean it. I know this is a big sacrifice, and I didn't want you to have to pull out of school and take time off from your studies. But I'm super grateful you did."

Julie pushed a forkful of eggs around on her plate. "I didn't take time off school just for you. Although I would, because I love you. But I'm feelin' kinda stuck. I couldn't focus. I needed a break."

"I'm sorry to hear that. Anything I can help you with?"

"No, there's nothin' anyone can do. This whole thing with Matilda has really shaken me up. I don't know what to do, who I am, or what to believe. It's like the whole world turned out to be a lie and I can't trust anyone. I'm in a slump, and I can't figure how to pull myself out of it."

"I didn't know you were feelin' that way," Rita said. She wanted so badly to fix everything for Julie. She'd raised her like her own daughter since Helen died, and they'd been through so many ups and downs in that time. The tumult of the teen years had drawn them closer together, if anything. All she wanted was to protect her from more heartache.

"I didn't want to bother you with my emotions. You've got enough going on in your own life."

Rita sighed. "I still want to know everything about you. I can multi-task."

Julie reached for Rita's hand and squeezed it. "I know you can."

"There's a simple way to figure this out — Matilda is living right next door with her new husband. You can call her up, or go over to see her. I'm sure she'd be more than happy to talk about it. It's been a bit of a rollercoaster ride for her as well."

Julie released Rita's hand. "I'm not ready to talk to her about it."

"You can't blame her, you know?" Rita said in a soft voice. "It's not her fault."

Julie's eyes flashed. "If she'd stayed in Australia and left us alone, we wouldn't have known, and we'd be fine."

"You'd rather not know?" Rita wasn't sure she could agree. Better to get the truth out into the open than live in ignorance —that had always been her policy.

"Yes, I would rather not know. I was happy. Well, happy enough, anyhow. I missed Mom, but I knew that she'd loved me. That you were my aunt. That Tyler and Sophie were my cousins. That Grandma and Grandpa were... " She stopped, her voice breaking on the words.

"We're still your family, honey. That won't change."

"You know it's not the same. It can't ever be the same again. And it's all her fault."

* * *

After breakfast, Julie cleaned up while Rita went in search of the key for the locked closet. She wanted to sort through it today, while she felt good. Who knew when she'd be well enough next to manage it?

It took a while to locate the key, but she finally found it in a small, creaky drawer in the antique coatrack by the front door. She unlocked the padlock on the closet and then pulled the door open, heard a bang, and immediately coughed as a cloud of dust enveloped her.

"Gracious! That's been shut too long," she muttered to herself.

After foraging in her own closet for a scarf to tie around her mouth, she returned and found the dust had settled. A stack of papers and magazines had fallen from the top of a filing cabinet to the floor, causing the commotion.

The closet was bigger than she'd remembered. She could walk all the way into it. There were shelves on either side and at the back, and every shelf was packed to the brim with stuff. Newspapers, magazines, paperwork, trinkets, books, albums, bags of clothing and a multitude of other things she'd have to dig through.

She found a chair in the den and pulled it into the closet. Then she sat down to weed through the piles of junk. Why had her parents filled this thing up and then locked it? Why hadn't she ever thought to clean it out? She hadn't wanted to disrupt what they'd stored away. She'd been busy, and truthfully, wasn't sure she'd be able to face it. But it seemed that having to look her own mortality in the eyes had given her a new stoicism. She wanted to reminisce over old photos and didn't find it hurtful any longer to see pictures of her parents. Enough time had passed, and she wasn't sure how many more years she'd have on this earth to share with loved ones even if memories were all she had of them.

There was a rocking horse stashed in the corner that she'd rocked on as a child and then her own children had as well. She'd thought her mother had gotten rid of it, but there it stood. A little worse for wear, but otherwise the same, with its green saddle and black mane. There was a photograph in a frame leaning against the shelves at the back of the space. Rita lumbered over to pick it up and dusted it off with a handker-chief from her pocket. There were her parents, squinting through the sunlight to smile at the camera. They stood on the dock, with Dad's beloved boat floating in the water behind them. Those were happy times. She smiled to herself, her throat tightening a little as memories washed over her.

Behind where the frame had sat was a large filing box. It was just as dusty as the frame. She tugged her chair closer and sat down, then pulled it towards herself. It was heavy, but not too bad. The lid was stuck, so it took a bit of work to get it free. Inside, she found several photo albums, and piles of letters tied together with white ribbon that had aged to a yellow colour.

She flicked through the envelopes with one finger, noting that they were from her parents to one another, or her grandmother and aunt to her father. The dates stamped on the outside of the envelopes suggested the letters had been written over many years, some from before they were married and some after. She was excited to read through them, but not now. Now she had to sort this entire room. And she wasn't sure how long her energy would last, so she'd better get going.

Chapter Five

The sound of birds outside her window pulled Matilda Berry-Merritt out of a deep slumber. At first she couldn't understand where the honking sound was coming from. Finally, her eyes blinked open, and she took in the room. She was lying in bed with her new husband in their house by Jackson Lake around fifty miles outside of Atlanta. And the honking was a goose flying overhead.

With a yawn, she rolled over towards him and was met with a barrage of kisses all over her face and gentle tickling of her ribs until she broke into gales of laughter. Then Ryan pulled her close into a warm hug. She snuggled against his chest.

"Good morning, wife," he said.

She yawned again. "Good morning, husband."

After a while, she got up and showered, then padded out to the kitchen where Ryan was stirring pancake batter while wearing nothing but a pair of boxer shorts. His muscular chest was tanned from working in the sun on the house renovations.

"Hungry?" he asked.

She nodded, searching through the fridge for bacon. She

set it on the counter and began frying it in batches. By the time the bacon was done, Ryan had a plate full of steaming hot pancakes ready for them to eat.

"There are only two of us," she joked.

He shrugged. "I'll freeze the leftovers and eat on them for the rest of the week."

"So efficient," she quipped as he tried to grab her. She spun past him with the plate of bacon and set it on the table with a laugh.

They sat down to eat together. Matilda slathered her pancakes with butter and syrup. She hadn't felt this happy in her entire life. The past months had been a roller coaster of emotions. She'd learned that her biological parents lived in the USA and weren't the couple who raised her in Australia. That she'd been swapped at a fertility clinic as an embryo with Julie, the woman whose aunt lived next door.

It was all very complicated and thinking about it made her head ache, not to mention her heart. She was still coming to terms with all of the implications of what she'd learned, and now that she and Ryan were married, she was beginning to realise she might not be going back home to Australia for a long while. He was embedded in Georgia, with his own construction company, a house and his extended family all close by. She missed her own family, who lived back in Brisbane. She'd begun to feel homesick, even though she was blissfully happy with her new husband and life.

"What do you have on today?" she asked.

Ryan swallowed a bite of pancakes. "I have to head to the site. The construction on the new strip mall is starting today."

"That's exciting."

He waggled his eyebrows. "Yes, it is. *Super* exciting."

She laughed. "I think it is. I've never worked on a construction site."

"Well, there'll be some digging today, but not much more than that. It'll be pretty dull. How about you?"

"I've got a shift at the café. Rita wants me to keep an eye on things. She has chemo. And Cathy is still learning, so someone has to be there to make sure she doesn't burn the place down." She was joking, but only sort of. Ever since Cathy had started working at the Honeysuckle Café, it'd been challenging dealing with her abrupt manner, her interference in every aspect of the business, and her overconfidence.

"How's it going with Cathy? Is everyone playing nice?"

"Amanda isn't a fan."

"Who's Amanda again?"

"She's the café manager, and sometimes the cook as well."

"So, it would be bad to annoy her."

Matilda nodded vigorously. "Yes, very bad. We need her. She's the glue that holds that place together most days, especially with Rita gone so much. Last week, Cathy told Amanda that the way she was seating people was too casual, that she could learn a few lessons from Miss Manners. And that the reason people were leaving without ordering dessert was because we're offering 'boring options.'"

Ryan laughed. "I'm sure Amanda loved that."

"Oh, yeah. She was thrilled. I thought her head would explode, her face was so red."

After breakfast, Matilda got dressed for work. She wore a pair of jeans and a buttoned black shirt. She'd add an apron when she arrived at the café, since she often moved between the kitchen and the customers, depending on where she was needed throughout the shift. They'd been low on cooks and kitchen hands lately, and she could easily plate meals, throw together salads, and so on.

Ryan called out a goodbye while she was still getting dressed. He'd been under a lot of pressure lately with his construction business. They'd taken on a big project, and he was spread thin. But they did their best to spend time together whenever they had the chance. And so far, she was loving married life. She couldn't quite believe they were married. They'd done it first out of convenience for her green card, but now they were living as a married couple and learning more about each other every day. It'd been an adventure, and one she still wasn't prepared for.

Her family were upset when she told them. Stella, her sister, had dreamed of being a bridesmaid since they were little kids. But there wasn't much Matilda could do about that now. Matilda's brothers had already forgotten that they were upset with her and had moved on. One of the advantages of having two brothers who were reasonably self-absorbed was that they didn't hold on to grudges very long.

Besides, she was deliriously happy. They couldn't stay mad at her for that. She knew that deep down, they all wanted her to be happy. But they missed her, and she missed them. She wished things could've gone differently. It wasn't as though she'd planned the whole thing—it just kind of happened.

On her way out the door, she dropped her keys in the mud. They still hadn't finished the landscaping around the house yet. The renovations Ryan had begun on their house by the lake were underway before she'd even met him. He said it sometimes felt as though it might never end.

He was used to managing construction crews rather than doing it all himself, but he enjoyed it, at least most of the time. He liked putting their home together with his own two hands. And it was almost done, but the mud around the outside of the house and down the walkways to where her car was parked was driving her crazy. She had to wear flip-flops to the car and then change into her shoes at work. She'd started calling thongs "flip-flops" because that's what Ryan called them.

With a grimace, she picked up the keys out of the mud, then tiptoed along the timber plank Ryan had laid out through the mud as a kind of footpath. When she reached her car, she sighed with relief and set her purse on the passenger seat. As she made her way around the outside of the vehicle, she spotted Julie sitting on the back porch of Rita's lake house next door. She raised a hand in greeting, giving a smile as well. Julie looked so much like Stella, it was easy to feel familiar with her, but Julie didn't respond. She'd clearly seen Matilda, but turned away to stare out over the water.

Matilda sat in the driver's seat, feeling a little deflated. She understood that Julie might not be ready to deal with the truth around their background, the fact that the two of them were raised in families across the world from their biological ties. But it hurt to think that she might blame Matilda for that. Matilda had hoped the two of them could be friends, could talk about their childhoods so she could learn as much as possible about her biological parents. And she was happy to tell Julie all about her own parents, but it seemed Julie wasn't interested in having anything at all to do with Matilda.

She started the car and set off towards the café. After she moved in with Ryan, he'd bought her a brand-new Toyota hybrid as a wedding gift. It was red and zippy, and she loved it. It was just like him to be so thoughtful and generous.

While she drove, she connected her phone to Bluetooth and called Rita.

"Hey, girl," Rita said. "Where are you?"

"I'm headed to the Honeysuckle. How about you?"

"At the hospital."

"Everything okay?"

"Yeah, I have another treatment today."

"Is Julie picking you up afterwards?"

"She is. She's been a big help lately. I couldn't do it without her."

Matilda hesitated. She didn't want to cause trouble, but

she had to ask Rita about Julie. "I saw her a few minutes ago, and she acted like I wasn't there."

Rita sighed. "I'm sorry, honey. She's a little het up about the whole IVF situation."

"I know—me too. But I really hope she gives me a chance sometime. I'd love to get to know her. Maybe even be friends."

"Give it time, hon. Just give it time. She'll come around. She's a sweetheart, but she has a lot on her mind right now. You know she left college?"

"I heard that."

"Right in the middle of her dissertation. And she's been working towards getting this degree for a long time. So, it's a pretty big deal, even if she's acting like it's not. The IVF news threw her for a loop, and I think she's still trying to find her feet. But in the meantime, she's taking me to treatments, keeping house, cooking and generally taking good care of me. I'm so grateful to her, but I don't want her to give up on her studies. She's worked so hard. I hope she goes back before too long."

"I'm sure she will," Matilda offered, although she had no way of knowing what Julie planned to do, since the woman wouldn't even talk to her. "Is there anything I can do to help?"

"You're already helping at the café for me. You're practically running the place."

"Well, not exactly running it." Matilda laughed. "At least, not according to Cathy."

Rita huffed. "Don't you worry about Cathy. She's going to be okay. But we need you at the Honeysuckle. It's my baby, and I feel better knowing you're there. You can't let Amanda and Cathy tear the place apart. You've got to keep the peace. Okay?"

"I'm doing my best," Matilda replied.

As she hung up the call, she couldn't help wondering how on earth she would be able to manage that.

Chapter Six

When Rita rolled out of bed the next morning, her feet bumped the box of letters and memorabilia she'd fished out of the storage closet a few days earlier. She'd been up late last night reading, and her eyes were still blurred with sleep when she pushed her reading glasses onto her nose again this morning to peer at the last letter she'd opened.

She yawned, then squinted.

Dear Ray,

The children and I are settled at Mom and Dad's place. I know you didn't want us to come here without you for so long, but I had to get away, and I hope you understand that. It's summer anyway, and the girls need something more to do than swim in the lake. Although they do love to do that.

The beach here is a little eroded this year. The last hurricane hit the North Carolina coast hard, especially the Outer Banks. But the girls don't seem to notice. They love it. They're taking the new sand bucket you bought them down to the water's edge each day to build castles.

Do you think that you and Bill will get through this? Do you think you can... I don't know ... move on?

It's a lot to ask, and I understand if you're still not ready to talk about it with me. But the silence was driving me mad. I couldn't stay any longer. You've got to say something eventually. Please.

Anyway, we're here for now. You know how to call or write. I hope you will.

With love from your wife,

Sylvia June Lambert

Rita had read it the previous evening, and it had hung heavy on her heart all night long. She'd tossed and turned and only managed to get into the lightest of sleeps for a short while. She vaguely remembered spending a large part of one summer with her grandparents in Rodanthe when she was about eight years old. But all that she could recall was fun in the sun, happy days playing in the sand, and her grandmother's home-made biscuits slathered in butter and jelly when they got back home each day.

She'd had no idea that her parents were going through something. And what were they going through? She couldn't say. Were they fighting? Or was it the conflict with Uncle Bill that left her father so quiet that her mother needed to find a place of escape?

Gently, she folded the letter back into its aged and fragile envelope and placed it to one side of the box. She'd already gone through a few of the letters, but most weren't particularly interesting. There was correspondence between her mother and an aunt who lived in Raleigh, but most of their ruminating was on the children—who was doing what and going where with whom and when. It was fun to remember. So many of the details had been lost with the passage of time—her memory felt more like flashes of familiarity these days, than of anything concrete.

She lumbered to her feet and had a leisurely hot shower. Then, after donning a long, flowing, flowery summer dress, she slipped her feet into a pair of sandals and wandered out to the kitchen, still scrunching the curls in her damp hair.

She'd hoped to find that Julie had gone out, since it was relatively late in the morning and she didn't want Julie to feel as though she had to hang around waiting for Rita to rise. Getting up early had been part of her normal routine, but it was getting harder with the treatments sucking every last remnant of energy from her body.

With a quick glance around, she soon realised the house was empty. So, she set the coffee to percolate while mixing up a batch of biscuits for the oven. There was some leftover sausage gravy from the day before, and she was hankering for a nice hot breakfast.

She poured herself a mug of steaming hot coffee, added a dash of vanilla creamer, and then headed for the back porch. It was then that she spotted Julie's brown head, barely visible above the back of the rocking chair. She poured another cup of coffee and carried it outside.

She pushed through the door. "What are you doing here?" She beamed at her niece and handed her the coffee.

Julie issued a tired smile. "Oh, there you are. News flash: I live here. I was wondering when you'd get out of bed, lazy bones. Thanks for the coffee."

Rita laughed. "I do feel lazy. It's a guilty kind of feeling, like there's something I should be doing when I don't rise with the dawn and head to the café."

"Well, enjoy it. You should lay in as much as you like. You've definitely earned that privilege, as hard as you work."

Rita sat in the rocking chair beside Julie's. "Thanks, honey. I'll get used to it, I guess."

"How're you doing?"

Rita shrugged. "As well as can be expected. I've been better. But I've been worse."

"Not nauseated?"

"A little. But I'm gonna try some biscuits and gravy—see if that helps."

"Sausage gravy. That's ambitious when you're feeling queasy. But I'm all for it."

Rita chuckled. "I was never one for half measures. Go the whole hog, I always say. There's more than enough, if you want some."

"That would be great. I haven't eaten yet. Didn't have much of an appetite when I got up this morning."

"And when was that?" Rita asked.

"Around four."

"Four in the morning?" Rita's eyebrows arched skyward. "Why on earth would you do a thing like that?"

Julie sighed. "I couldn't sleep any longer. I've been so restless lately. My heart was racin', and there was this anxious feeling in my gut. It's settled a little now."

Rita worried about her niece. She'd never seen her like this before—despondent, low energy. Usually, Julie was outgoing, bubbly, ready for the next challenge to come her way. And always working towards a goal. For years, that goal had been to become a psychologist. Now, she'd given up on that dream, hopefully only temporarily, but it was hard to say.

"How are you doin', honey?" Rita's voice was soft and warm.

"I'm okay. I'm more worried about you." Julie reached over to pat Rita's arm.

"I know you are, but I'm going to be just fine."

"We're going to make sure of it." Julie gave her a tight smile.

"I worry that you've given up on your dreams." Rita didn't want to say it. Almost as if she uttered the words, it would make them true. But she had to know. She couldn't stand by and let Julie suffer silently.

Julie's eyes reddened. "I haven't given up. Not really. But the problem is, I don't know what my dreams are anymore."

"Yes, you do," Rita objected. "You've always known what you wanted."

"I always knew who I was, as well. Now, I'm not so sure."

"Nothing has changed..." Rita began. But it wasn't true. Everything had changed, and she didn't know how to fix it.

Chapter Seven

Around lunchtime, Julie drove Rita to the hospital. They used Julie's car, since it was a small hatchback with air-conditioning, leather seats, and Bluetooth. Much more comfortable than Rita's old truck with the stubborn stick shift and the unreliable air.

Julie still felt hung over from the lack of sleep. She sat in the waiting room, hunched in her chair with Rita beside her. Before long, a lovely nurse strode out to greet them and take them back to see the doctor before the treatments began for the day. Julie was surprised when she glanced at the door to see the name *Dr James Fuller, MD* mounted there. Still gaping, she stepped into the room and found herself staring at James, seated behind a large mahogany desk. He came to greet them and ushered them into chairs facing his.

"Good to see you again, Rita, Julie. How are you feeling, Rita?"

Julie interrupted. "You're Rita's doctor?"

"Her oncologist, yes. You didn't know that?" His blue eyes were piercing against the dark wall behind him.

"No, I didn't realise. Wow."

"You know each other?" Rita asked, a bemused expression on her face.

Julie felt as though her cheeks might burst into flames. "James lived with me and Mom a long time ago. Don't you remember?"

Recognition dawned. Rita's eyes widened. "James? Oh, heavens! I didn't put that together. Of course I remember. You were shorter then, although not much. But you've changed a bunch."

James laughed. "I hope so. I was only fifteen at the time."

"Well, I'll be… That's something." Rita grinned. "How are you, James?"

"I'm well, thanks. But I'm going to turn it back to you, since you're the patient here."

Rita inhaled a slow breath. "I'm okay. Not feeling great. I've been nauseated and tired. I threw up last night."

"I didn't know that." Julie frowned at her.

Rita patted her leg. "It's okay, honey. This is all part of it."

"I can give you something for the nausea. Just keep a log of any symptoms you're feeling so we can make sure we stay on top of things."

"Will do," Rita replied.

As Julie sat and listened to the exchange, she was suddenly aware of just how much of a mess she was. She'd run a comb through her hair that morning, then piled it in a messy bun on top of her head. But other than that, she'd made no effort with her normally immaculate appearance. Usually she dressed up for life on campus, but this morning she'd thrown on shorts, a T-shirt, and some sandals. No makeup, her self-tan had faded weeks ago, and her nails were short and chipped. She'd given up on any kind of beauty routine when she left college. But with James seated behind his desk, hair perfectly combed, skin glowing and wearing an expensive shirt and slacks beneath his long white coat, she felt very out of place.

"I'm going to wait outside," she said, rising to her feet.

Rita nodded and Julie rushed out the door, aiming for the waiting room. She stood there for a few moments, looking around. The place was packed. Then, she went to the bathroom to splash water on her face. Maybe it would wake her up a little, help with the bags beneath her eyes.

Even after that, she still felt like the air was stifling, so she hurried out through the double automatic doors. As she stepped outside, she twisted an ankle and almost landed in a heap on the sidewalk. Thankfully, she was able to catch herself and steady her gait, but the pain was enough to make her yelp. There was no one close by to hear it, and a steady stream of traffic on the road so that any noise she made was quickly drowned out. But she glanced around just in case she'd drawn any attention. Satisfied that she hadn't completely embarrassed herself, she found a bench to sit on and lowered herself tentatively onto it. Then she raised her foot to her other knee so she could massage her ankle.

"Are you okay?"

James had followed her outside. He squatted in front of her, a concerned look on his face.

She forced a smile. "I'm fine. Really, you should go back inside and take care of Aunt Rita."

"She's started on her treatment. I'm free for a few minutes." He sat on the bench beside her. "You seem a little down. Anything wrong?"

"I'm worried about Aunt Rita."

"I can understand that."

Julie studied him. His blue eyes were fixed on hers, deep and intense. "It's been so long since we've seen each other. What have you been up to?" It was all she could think to say.

"After I left your house, I moved to Alabama with Mom. We did okay there, although I missed home. I missed you two as well. And I didn't make friends easily there—I found it hard to fit in. I decided that in order to get out of there, I needed good grades, so that became my focus. I was obsessed, and it paid off. I got into Emory and studied medicine. Now, here I am."

"I can't believe we never heard from you again."

"I spoke to Helen every now and then. She helped me a time or two."

"Really? I didn't know that."

"Yeah, she was great. Your mom meant a lot to me. I was sad to hear she'd passed. I wanted to come to the funeral, but I wasn't able to get there in time."

"That's okay. It was a lovely service. I wish you could've been there."

"I'm sure you miss her."

"So much. Every day." She rubbed a hand over her face. The thought came unbidden—*but she wasn't my mother*. She didn't want to think those things, but it happened all the time. The thought would pop into her head and there it would stay, hanging around like a bad scent. Would she ever come to terms with what she'd learned?

"Well, I'm glad I got to see you again. I've wondered for years what happened to you, what you were doing. So, are you living nearby?"

"I *was* studying psychology at UGA, but I'm taking a break to look after Aunt Rita."

"Oh, wow. That's kind of you. It's a good idea."

"It is?"

"Of course, she needs you. And it can be hard to focus when someone we care about is sick. This way you can give your attention to Rita and not lose sight of your goal. You can go back to it when you're ready and refreshed to start again."

"You're right—that does sound like a good idea. Much better than me flunking out because I couldn't handle the pressure of it all."

He laughed. "I doubt that was the case. I remember you being great under pressure."

It was so nice to talk to someone who knew her, really knew her, had seen her as a kid. Who knew what she was capable of and that she wasn't one to give up. Tears pricked in her throat.

"Thanks, James. Seeing you again is almost like therapy." She issued a hollow laugh. "And I can't afford therapy."

"Soon you'll be able to give yourself therapy," he quipped.

She huffed. "I'll never get anything else done."

He chuckled. "Hey, I've got to get back to work, but I'd love to catch up some more. Can I get your number?"

She nodded. "Sure, that would be really nice. I don't know a lot of people around the area these days. I've been living in Athens for years."

"Perfect. I don't know many people because all I do is work, so we can get together and moan about our lack of friends."

"Sounds good."

She gave him her number, and he waved as he walked back through the hospital doors. She caught herself smiling even after he was gone. She already felt better than she had before. There was something truly soothing about him. He'd been that way as a teenager as well. She liked being around him, and it certainly didn't hurt that he looked good in a white coat. She only wished she'd had the foresight to dress a little more stylishly. Although, truth be told, she wasn't sure she had the energy for it. Right now, it was all she could do to get out of bed and drag herself through each day. With a sigh, she got to her feet and hobbled back inside to find Rita.

Chapter Eight

Matilda's long blonde hair was pulled back into a ponytail so she could focus on the job at hand. She was gap filling. It wasn't a very important job, but Ryan assured her it was necessary and would help him with the painting. They were so close to finishing their home renovations, and she couldn't wait until it was finally done. She used the word "they" loosely, since it was really Ryan who'd done most of the work. Selfishly, she wanted him to herself when he came home, so she was ready for him to be finished with this seemingly never-ending job.

She squinted and reached above the doorframe to fill a gap with the caulking gun.

"You do that so well," Ryan said as he leaned lazily against the wall, a nail gun pointed at the floor beside his feet. He grinned her and winked.

She laughed. "Thank you. I've become something of an expert. I *have* been doing it now for almost two hours, you know."

"I'll have to hire you for the jobsite."

She smirked, then grew thoughtful as she filled another

gap with the caulk gun. "I've been thinking about changing direction, actually."

"You're not going to become a construction worker now, are you?" He grinned.

She shook her head. "I love working at the café, but I miss being a vet. I think I needed a break from it. And now that I've had some time off, I miss working with animals."

"I can understand that," Ryan said, coming over to wrap his arms around her gently.

She leaned into his chest. "I miss home, too."

"We should visit sometime."

"Yeah, but when?"

"Maybe we could go at Christmas. I'll have some time off then."

"Okay, that sounds good. I'd like that."

"And you should look into vet jobs here. If that's what you want to do."

She sighed. "I'm concerned about Rita and the café, though. She needs me there while she's going through treatment."

He nodded and squeezed her. "You're good to her."

"I try to be. She's my aunt, after all."

"I'm sure she appreciates what you're doing."

"She does. She tells me all the time. So, I can't abandon her. I've got to stay at the café until she's ready to take over working there again. I'm helping her keep an eye on Cathy."

"It makes sense for you to stay at the café, but maybe you could look around and see what opportunities are out there so you're ready when Rita feels better."

"You're right. I'll do that. Thanks." The thought of getting back into her old career path sent a thrill of excitement running through her veins. She'd been burned out and needed a break when she first travelled to the USA. But now, she was ready to get back into it.

Chapter Nine

The next day, Rita felt up to visiting the café. There were some accounts she wanted to go over, so she snuck through the back entrance and settled into her office after the lunch crowd had died down. The Honeysuckle Café was thriving with a full breakfast and lunch service. They'd added a dinner menu about five years earlier, and it was building momentum as well. Every now and then, they held a party or special event to boost the numbers, and it seemed as though the locals were finally ready to embrace the café as a dinner option.

There was a stack of envelopes on Rita's desk—most were bills she had to pay. She gradually sifted through the pile, reading each one in turn and either adding it to the trash can, the bills pile, or the deal-with-later pile.

An hour later, she was exhausted and ready to go home, but that was when Cathy found her. She barged into the office with a frown, then drew up short when she saw Rita sitting there.

"Oh...Rita. I didn't know you were in here. I'm looking for tape."

"What kind of tape?"

"Something to hold the leg of a chair together."

"How about duct tape?"

"That might do it. Why are you here?"

Rita laughed. "That's a nice hello."

"You know what I mean."

"I'm paying some bills. They never stop, unfortunately. How're y'all doin' today?"

Cathy sat in the chair across from Rita's desk, its back pushed up against the wall because the office was tiny. There was barely enough room for the two of them, a desk, a computer and a filing cabinet.

"It's been busy this mornin'. I told y'all we shouldn't have added the French toast to the breakfast menu. We had so many orders that we ran out, and then Russ had to make more, which put us behind…"

Rita laughed. "That's a good thing, honey. That's what we want—people linin' up for our French toast."

Cathy pouted. "It put a lot of pressure on us. I was waitin' tables, washing dishes, running around like the place was on fire."

Rita shook her head slowly. "Lord have mercy! Sounds like you had a normal day working at a busy café, honey. That's how it is 'round here."

"You don't have to be patronisin'." Cathy crossed her arms. "You always do that. So smug. One day, you'll see what it's like…"

"What does that mean?" Rita's eyes narrowed.

"Nothing. It doesn't mean anythin'. Only I wish you wouldn't treat me like a child." Her lips protruded forwards, and Rita had to resist the urge to point out that her current behaviour was a little childish. She didn't want to provoke her cousin further. She wanted a detente, peace.

"I'm sorry, honey. I never mean to do that."

Cathy's blue eyes filled with tears, and she tucked a loose

strand of grey-blonde hair behind one ear. "You don't know what it's like to be me."

"Of course I don't." Rita drew a slow breath and released it to calm her nerves. The stress of everything lately had her wound up and spinning like a top. Sometimes it helped her to remember that others were going through their own things as well. "What's happenin', hon?"

Cathy pulled a tissue from her sleeve and dabbed her heavily made-up eyes with it. "You know Gareth and I have been going through some hard times."

"I *didn't* know that. I'm sorry to hear it."

"Well, he moved out a few months ago. Right before I came to see you the first time. I didn't want to say anythin', because it's a private matter, but we're separated." Tears sparkled in her eyes, and she dabbed them away again.

Rita's heart filled with compassion for her difficult and headstrong cousin. "That's a hard thing you're going through."

"It's been horrible. And it's exactly why I came to the café to see you. I wanted to be part of something. To have a connection to my parents. They're gone now, but I miss them every day. Never more so than when Gareth walked out on me. I wanted to talk to them so bad..." She burst into tears, pressing the tissue to her face and sobbing violently into it.

Rita got up and lumbered around the desk to pat her on the back. It was awkward, but she wasn't sure exactly how to comfort her cousin, who usually bristled at any signs of affection.

After a while, Cathy's tears calmed. Rita went back to her seat and pulled the old photographs she'd been looking at a few days earlier from her desk drawer. She set them on the desk and pushed them across to Cathy.

"Take a look at these."

There were photographs of Cathy's parents along with

Rita's. The kids were there too, with a tiny Cathy clinging to her mother's leg and grinning wide. It looked as though both Rita and Cathy had something dark around their mouths in another photograph—possibly ice cream or maybe chocolate. It was hard to say, but both looked particularly pleased with themselves in the image.

Cathy flipped through the photographs. She smiled, then she laughed, and finally she set them down and met Rita's gaze.

"Thanks for that. It was exactly what I needed."

"Why didn't you say anything before now?" Rita asked.

Cathy blinked back tears. "We have a… complicated relationship, you and I."

"You can say that again." Rita laughed. "But I hope you know you can always talk to me. About anything, really. I'm here for you."

"I know what you think of me. I can see it in your eyes. You think I'm a joke." Cathy sniffled.

"I don't think you're a joke. We don't always get along, it's true. And sometimes you frustrate me—I'll be the first to admit to that. But I still care about you. You're my cousin. We grew up runnin' around this place together. We caused a lot of mischief for our parents, the two of us."

"I remember." Cathy smiled. "Do you recall that one summer day when we filled water balloons and threw them at our dads when they came out of the café into the courtyard? They were so mad."

Rita laughed. "I thought they were going to tan our hides. But then they grabbed the ones that didn't burst and threw them right back at us."

"That was a good day." Cathy wiped the tears from her cheeks. "I miss it — all of it."

"Me too." Rita sighed. "But things will get better. I'm sure they will."

"And for you too," Cathy replied.

"Thanks, I appreciate that. How are you doin' here? Is the café working out for you?"

Cathy straightened in her chair. "Amanda is difficult…"

"She's amazing at what she does. She doesn't much like change, but she's doing pretty well, considering."

"She doesn't like being told what to do. That's what it is."

"Well, she's the manager around here, so for now, you should probably listen to her rather than coming up with stuff for her to do."

"But I'm…"

"You're a guest here, Cathy. I'm the owner, Amanda is the manager, and you're here at my request to see how you get along. I'm sorry if that upsets you, but it's how it has to be for now. We can't have our staff getting torn apart because you're throwin' your weight around."

"I'm not doing that." She sniffed.

"I'm only askin' you to think before you speak. You're new to the café business. Amanda has far more experience. She knows what she's doing. Let her lead, and you'll find your way."

She was pouting. "Is that ever going to change? Will you ever see me as more than a guest around here?"

Rita leaned forward. "It's up to you. I don't know what the future holds, but I do know that I love this café. It's a part of me, and I care what happens to it. I've invited you to be here, but I need to see that you feel the same way about it, that you care what happens to it, and that includes the staff."

"I do care."

"Then show me."

Chapter Ten

The sun had dropped towards the tree line during Julie's walk around Jackson Lake. She'd driven Rita to her appointment at the hospital earlier, and they'd just gotten home in time for Rita to have a lie down. So, before she made dinner, Julie decided to take a walk. She'd been walking daily since she moved into the lake house and found that it helped to calm her anxiety and to process all of the thoughts racing through her mind.

It was quiet, peaceful. Birds called. Occasionally a car crept by on the winding road, but otherwise, she was mostly alone. And she liked it that way. It gave her a chance to let her thoughts wander. But the danger in that was, inevitably questions rose to the surface like, *What am I doing with my life? Will I go back to my studies? Will I ever finish? What if I don't want to be a psychologist after all this work?*

And when that happened, she had to push those thoughts aside and intentionally focus on the water lapping at the lake's edge, or a trail of ducklings paddling behind their green-and-brown mother. Anything to stop the rising panic and the heart palpitations from worsening.

Her phone rang, and she tugged it from her pocket. The number wasn't familiar. Maybe she should let it go to voicemail. But what if it was important? She answered, bracing herself to hang up on a spam caller. But instead, she heard a familiar voice.

"Hi, Julie. It's James."

A broad smile spread across her lips. "James, how're you doing?"

"I'm well. And you?"

"I'm takin' a stroll around the lake. It's beautiful at this time of day."

"That sounds nice. I'm finishing up my shift at the hospital, but I wanted to call and see if you're free for dinner. I know it's last minute, so I understand if you're busy."

She hadn't expected that. In fact, the phone call had surprised her. Even though she'd given him her phone number, she'd anticipated that he'd be far too busy to think about her, let alone call. Seeing him again reminded her of how much she'd enjoyed that period of her life when he was a temporary part of their little family. "That would be lovely. I don't have any plans."

They arranged that he would pick her up, and she hurried back to the lake house to fix a quick meal for Rita, shower and change. She wore a long green halter dress with the gold necklace Aunt Rita had given her at Christmas. It had a gold heart strung on it, and already it was sentimental to Julie. Everything felt sentimental these days. Her emotions were close to the surface. She felt somewhat numb, but at the same time, any little thing brought tears to her eyes.

She wasn't sure how this would go and was a little nervous about catching up with James again after all this time. It was awkward enough at the hospital—now she had to make a conversation with him last through an entire meal. What would they have in common other than that brief time they lived together? And to be honest, most of that period was a bit of a blur to her these days. She'd been pretty young and hadn't paid too much attention to the gangly teenaged boy her mother took in other than to initially be annoyed by him and then to gradually realise he was kind of nice and she liked spending time with him. But then he'd moved out. And, after a while, she only thought of him every now and then. She'd wondered several times in recent years what had happened to him.

Rita was watching television when Julie came out, a cup of soup on the small table beside her armchair.

"I found my soup, thanks. You look pretty," Rita said. "Going somewhere special?"

"James asked me to dinner."

"James?"

"I mean, Dr Fuller." Her cheeks warmed.

Rita smiled. "*My* Dr Fuller?"

"Uh-huh. It's not going to be weird, is it?" She wrung her hands together. "Because I can cancel if you're uncomfortable."

"Cancel? No, not a chance. I think it's great. He's a good man. And it's about time you had some fun."

A car pulled into the driveway, its tyres crackling on the gravel. The sun had dipped beyond the horizon now, so the headlights brightened the front yard.

"Have fun, honey!" Rita called as Julie dashed to the front door, her heart thudding.

James knocked and Julie opened the door immediately, surprising him. "Oh, hi. That was fast."

She laughed. "I saw the car lights." She shut the door behind her.

"Ready to go?"

She nodded. "Let's go."

He opened the car door for her, and she slid into the

passenger seat. Was this a date? It felt more like a date than a catch-up. He was dressed in a buttoned shirt and nice jeans, with his hair combed neatly. She was in a dress and heels. There was a definite tension in the air. It seemed date-like. She wasn't sure how she felt about that, although the buzz of excitement in her gut indicated she wasn't against the idea. It was strange to go on a date with a man who'd been like a brother to her at one point in her childhood, although that was a long time ago.

There was country music playing on the radio. She tapped her fingers on the seat beside her as he pulled the car back onto the street.

"Do you like country?" he asked.

She nodded. "I'm a Southerner. I don't have much of a choice."

He laughed. "I know what you mean."

The restaurant he chose was a BBQ place she'd been wanting to try. She'd driven past it a dozen times and read the sign. The scents that wafted out into the parking lot were delicious. The hostess led them to a table in the back and handed them each a menu. The place was packed, although not too loud. Especially where they were seated. It felt cozy and welcoming.

She decided on the Brunswick stew with corn bread, and he got a pulled pork sandwich with fries. Both of them ordered sweet tea although she added a glass of red wine as well, hoping the drink might help calm her nerves.

Finally, settled with their drinks, she sipped and slowly felt the anxiety dissipate as he chatted about work, the weather, and what he'd done on the weekend. She asked a few questions and then relaxed, listening to him speak. He had a nice voice, and he peppered his stories with funny anecdotes that soon had her in stitches. She'd forgotten he could be funny.

"And what about you? What have you been up to? I mean,

I know you've taken a break from college but what do you spend your days doing?"

This was the question she dreaded these days. She hadn't been up to anything. There was nothing interesting going on in her life at all. She was a homebody, a college drop-out who spent her days cleaning, cooking and generally taking care of her aging aunt. It was very glamorous.

"Well... I cleaned the kitchen. That was a huge undertaking, let me tell you." She cleared her throat and looked to see if the waitress was bringing their meal. "And I drove Aunt Rita to the hospital earlier. But you already knew that."

He nodded. "It must be a strange season of life. You were so busy with college, and now you're feeling less structured."

She huffed. "You can say that again. It's like I'm floating around in no particular direction. I feel lost and confused. I'm sure that sounds ridiculous to someone like you, who has their entire life planned out and every second of the day accounted for. But this is where I am right now."

"I hope this isn't too intrusive, but what made you lose your direction?"

Did she want to answer? She pursed her lips, thinking. "It's a really long story..."

"I've got plenty of time."

So, she told him all of it. How Matilda had come to visit, the news she'd brought with her. How it had torn Julie's entire world apart when Matilda revealed that the two of them had been switched as embryos at an IVF clinic. How she'd never get to meet her biological parents, and how Matilda now lived next door with her green-card husband.

"Wow. I was not expecting that," James said when she was done, blinking.

"Are you sorry you asked?"

He shook his head. "Definitely not sorry, but surprised.

You've been dealing with a lot. No wonder you needed to take some time out. Anyone would."

"Do you think so? I've been feeling like I'm a weakling. Like... why couldn't I just handle it? Why couldn't I take it? Why has it shaken me so much? I lost both my parents... the people who raised me. I pulled through that tragedy and kept marching, was on my way to making something of my life. I was always conscientious, hardworking, driven. But now... now I'm free-falling."

The waitress brought their meals and set the steaming plates down in front of them, then topped up their drinks. Before they ate, James reached across the table to squeeze her hand briefly before letting go.

"You have to give yourself time to come to terms with all of this. It's not a weakness to take the time you need. I think it shows a lot of wisdom, actually. To say to yourself, 'I'm not coping with this, and I think it's best I take a sabbatical to think it through, process it, figure out who I am now.' You've not only had a loss—you've taken a blow to your identity, the core of who you are."

Her throat tightened, and a lump formed. He understood. He saw her. "Yes! That's it. I don't know who I am anymore. Or whose I am. My family... isn't my family. I know they wouldn't agree with that. They say nothing has changed, but it has. It's all different now. And there's this whole other family on the other side of the world who I haven't met. I don't know if I want to meet them. I didn't want any of this. I still can't believe Matilda did this to me. She dropped a bomb, blew up my life, and then moved in next door!"

James sighed. "You must be really angry with her."

"I am!" she cried. "No one else seems to get that, so thank you for saying it. I'm angry. I'm so angry with her. How could she do this to me?"

Tears welled in her eyes, but she fought them back. He was

going to think she was a crazy person, bursting into tears over dinner. But she wasn't the type to cry. She hadn't cried in years. Not until recently, anyway. Not until Matilda.

He offered her a sympathetic look. "It'll get better. I promise it will."

She pressed both hands to her face. "I don't know if it will. I can't see a way forward. I need to *do* something. But I don't know what. I don't want to go back to college. Not yet, and I'm not sure if that will change. All I know is, I've got to get out of the house, at least for a little while, or I'll go crazy. I'm a doer, an achiever, and all I've got going on right now is puttering around and making sweet tea and biscuits for Aunt Rita. As much as I love her, I need more than that. But I can't bring myself to commit to anything more. I'm a basket case."

He shook his head. "You're not a basket case. You're dealing with something really hard. I'd be a mess if I were you."

They started to eat. Her stew was delicious, especially after she added some hot sauce. "I can't tell you how good it is to have someone to talk to. I can't discuss this with Rita because Matilda is her niece and Rita adores her. She can't understand why I don't want to besties with her." She issued a hollow laugh. "But I can't even talk to Matilda right now. I know it's not her fault. It makes no sense to be angry with her. She's gone through the same things I'm facing. But I do blame her —I can't help it. She could've just stayed put and kept it to herself, and I'd never have known."

"But would that be better?" he asked.

"Yes! I had a connection to my parents, even though they were gone. Now even my memories of my mother are tainted. And my relationships with Rita and the rest of my family are all coloured by this huge elephant in the room."

After they'd changed the subject, Julie realised she felt lighter, more at ease, as though a burden had lifted from her shoulders just by talking about her issues. She chatted and laughed more easily and felt more relaxed than she had in weeks.

"Where are your family from? The ones on the other side of the world?"

"Australia! Can you believe it? I've always wanted to go there, and now I have family there." She laughed. "It's where I'm from. Well, kind of. My heritage."

"Australia? Wow, that's so cool. I'm going there next week, actually."

"You're going next week? To Australia?" Her brow furrowed. "On vacation?"

"No, I have a conference for work. We're supposed to go to a conference for educational purposes every year, and this year I chose a symposium in Australia. It's on the Gold Coast, which sounds nice. I'm not sure how much time I'll have for sightseeing. Still, I'm excited. Gives me a change of pace from the grind of the hospital day after day."

"I'm so jealous. Even though I'm nervous to meet my family, I kind of desperately want to at the same time. Who knows when I'll ever get to go. At the rate of my career trajectory, maybe I'll get to visit them when I'm sixty." She laughed and popped some corn bread in her mouth.

"Come with me then," he said suddenly.

She almost choked. "Huh?"

He shrugged. "I was going with a colleague, but he backed out at the last minute and we can't get a refund on his tickets. Come with me. I'll switch the ticket to your name. You can travel with me, and then while I'm at the symposium, you can visit your family. It's already paid for, and it was just going to waste. You could use it instead."

She gaped at him. "You're serious?"

"Sure. Why not? It'll be a lot more fun with you there. I miss you. I didn't realise how much until tonight, but it's been really great catching up. I'd love to have more time together. And as I said, everything's already paid for…business class."

It was a crazy idea. She couldn't do that, could she? Drop everything and go to the other side of the world in one week? She tried to think of a single reason why to turn him down, but she had no commitments. Rita had finished her round of treatments. Julie didn't have school, or a job, or even friends to hang out with. She was completely free, as was the trip. And it would be stupid to pass up an all-expenses-paid vacation in Australia. Especially when it might mean she could connect with her sister and brothers. Even thinking about it sent a thrill down her spine.

"Yes, okay, I'll do it. I'll come to Australia with you."

Chapter Eleven

The café was filling up with the afternoon crowd. There was always a rush of customers around two to three o'clock when caffeine withdrawals kicked in. And Matilda was grateful for it. There was nothing worse than a slow shift. She much preferred to be run off her feet at the café. It made the time go fast, and she enjoyed the interactions with customers as well. She loved the Southern culture of conversing with the server. Or, as she'd call it in Australia, "having a chat." She'd gotten to know a lot of the regulars that way.

"You want a slice of pie this afternoon, Ken?" she asked one of those regulars.

Ken came in every day around the same time. He'd order a coffee, get out his iPad, and read up on the news. One of the reasons she liked him so well, was because he was a veterinarian too and they often shared funny stories with one another. He looked like he was coming up on retirement age and had probably slowed down in recent years. The two of them often sat and talked about their lives, if there weren't many other customers for her to take care of.

"Whaddya got?" He grinned, his glasses sliding down his

nose as they always did. He shoved them back with his forefinger.

"We have pecan, with a scoop of vanilla ice cream on the side. Perfect for a hot day."

"You've twisted my arm. I'll have that plus my usual coffee, thanks."

"Coming right up." Matilda hurried to place the order, then glanced around, looking for Rita. She hadn't been into the café much lately, but she was supposed to be there today. Matilda had seen her old truck parked outside, so she had to be there somewhere. Most probably in her office. She delivered Ken's order to him, then tidied up the pile of magazines on the coffee table near the front of the cafe.

She hadn't seen Rita for a few days and missed her. She wanted to talk to her about the idea going back to working as a vet. If she were to leave the café anytime in the near future, she really should give Rita as much warning as possible. And if Rita baulked at the idea, Matilda would drop it. She couldn't bear to hurt Rita if she could help it. But if Rita was okay with it, Matilda really wanted to get started. Ever since she'd first told Ryan that she might consider getting back into her own field, the prospect had been simmering and growing in her mind until she could barely think about anything else.

With a quick glance around the café, she noted that everyone seemed to be taken care of for the moment, so she scurried to the back of the building, where Rita's office was tucked away beside the kitchen. She knocked quietly, then pushed the door open.

"Rita?"

"Come on in, honey. I'd get up to give you a hug, but my legs are worn out."

Matilda went around the desk to kiss Rita's cheek. "No need—I'll come to you. How are you feeling?"

"I've felt better, let me tell you! But I'm survivin' each

day, and that's something to be grateful for. Besides, I finished my round of treatments, so I've got a little break before the next round starts. And that's another thing I can thank the Almighty for. I'm counting every blessing these days."

"That's a great perspective. I should do that more often myself. An attitude of gratitude really seems to help me when I'm feeling low."

"It sure does. Now, what can I do for you, honey? Everything okay out there in the café?"

"Everything's fine. We have a pretty full house, but it's all under control."

"Glad to hear it. How's Cathy doin', do you think?"

Matilda hesitated and drew a short breath. "Cathy's fine. She's improving. In fact, I spoke to her a few minutes ago and she seemed almost friendly, so maybe she's finally settling in."

"That *is* good to hear." Rita leaned back in her chair, eyes sparkling. "Keep me updated on that one." She groaned suddenly and pressed a hand to her forehead. "This headache is killin' me today. I can't concentrate."

Matilda opened her mouth to talk about her plans for the future, but decided against it. Rita wasn't feeling well. She was pale, looked weak, and was struggling.

"You should go home. Whatever you're doing can wait, can't it?"

"Well, I suppose you're right." Rita glanced at the computer screen with a frown.

"You need to get your rest. You're trying to do too much. The treatment round might be over, but you've still got to recover from it. Give yourself time. Maybe take a nap, get something to eat. You really haven't been holding down much food lately. Now's your chance to eat something delicious and actually get to enjoy it."

"That's a good point. I could do with a burger. A nice

juicy one, with tomato and lettuce." Rita licked her lips. "Just as soon as I get some Tylenol in me."

"I'll wrap up a burger for you while you gather your things. How does that sound?"

"It sounds perfect. Thank you, honey. I don't know what I'd do without you."

"Well, you don't have to worry about that," Matilda said with a pang of guilt.

She helped Rita to her feet, then returned to the kitchen to order a burger and fries with extra pickles on the side, just how Rita liked it. After Rita left, she got back to serving customers. When she took a coffee refill over to Ken's table, he glanced up from his iPad with a furrowed brow. "I was beginning to think I'd have to hunt you down."

She laughed. "I'm so sorry, Ken. I got caught up helping Rita. She's headed home now."

"How's she doing?"

"Pretty well, considering. Although she's a little tired."

"Well, tell her I said hi."

"I will. I was going to talk to her something, but I couldn't bring myself to do it. I hate to upset her."

His eyebrows arched, and he patted the empty chair beside him. "Tell me all about it."

Matilda checked that no other customers needed her, then slumped into the chair. "I guess I can sit for a few minutes."

"What's going on?" he asked.

"You know how I used to work as a veterinarian?"

"I still think you should go back to it."

"I've started thinking about doing just that. The problem is, I've never worked as a vet in this country, and I don't know what I'd have to do to get my license here."

"I'm sure it's only paperwork. Couldn't be too arduous." He took a bite of pie.

"You're probably right. At least, I hope you are."

"Do you know if you want to work for someone, or buy your own clinic? Because I don't have an opening in my team right now, but something might come up in the future. I could keep you in mind, if you like."

Matilda blinked. "Wow, thanks." She hadn't really thought that far ahead. She'd never owned her own clinic, but she'd dreamed that one day she would. "I'm not sure which way I'll go. I'd probably work for someone. I wouldn't even know where to start with my own clinic."

"Well, let me know what you decide. I have a friend who's retiring and selling his clinic. He's selling the whole thing, with equipment, staff, and everything. And he's doing it for a pretty good price because the place needs fixing up. He's ready to move on."

"That does sound interesting," she replied.

"I'll write down his number for you. You can give him a call if you want to find out more."

As she walked away from his table, she stared at the name and number on the napkin in her hands. Excitement buzzed in her gut. Could she do it? Could she purchase a clinic and run it herself? She had no experience managing staff, or a large budget, for that matter. She wasn't sure she'd even know what was involved in the day-to-day operations of a business. But she'd worked at veterinary clinics as a member of the staff for years. She was familiar with that side of things, even if she didn't know how to read a balance sheet (she'd tried once) or how to do payroll. Surely she could figure those things out. It couldn't be too hard. Still, was it what she wanted? There'd be a lot of work involved.

She took more coffee orders and handed them to the barista, as her thoughts flew. She could be a vet again — she loved working with animals. And maybe she could even run her own business. It was an exciting prospect. And a little scary too. But she wasn't one to veer away from something simply because it was frightening.

Chapter Twelve

Before long, Rita went home from the café. She was exhausted to her very bones. She hadn't felt this tired... well, ever. It was all catching up with her. The treatments, the business, the stress of family drama and the unraveling of so many things she'd thought were true. She'd held it together through Matilda's revelations, but if she gave herself a moment to be honest, it had devastated her at a deeper level.

The fact that Julie wasn't who she'd thought all these years was hard for her to accept. She knew it didn't really matter—Julie was still Julie. But it knocked the wind from her lungs when she let herself ponder it on the drive home. She felt small in the driver's seat, she didn't often feel small, but lately her weight had plummeted and her skin felt loose.

The house was quiet. She padded to the bedroom and lay down without changing. She kicked off her shoes, and they thudded one by one to the floor. Then she closed her eyes and fell into a deep sleep. She dreamed of the past—when her parents were young and vibrant, and her sister was with her, hand in hand. They explored the lake shore and found small birds eggs in a little nest buried in tall grass and reeds. Helen wanted to take them home to see if they could hatch them under a lamp, but Rita told her no. The birds needed their folks, just like human kids did.

When her eyes blinked open, there were tears on her cheeks. She shut them again, willing herself back to that happy place. But it was no use—she was awake now. It was darker in the bedroom, which mean the sun was close to setting. She got up and splashed water on her face. She felt drugged, but better. She must've slept for hours.

Julie was in the kitchen making dinner with a white apron covered in red flowers tied neatly around her trim waist. That apron hadn't fit Rita in years.

"Something smells 'bout good enough to eat," she said, sniffing the air.

Julie smiled. "Country fried chicken with greens and mashed potatoes."

"Music to my ears." Rita sat with a sigh in a chair at the kitchen table.

"You slept well," Julie remarked as she mashed the potatoes.

"I slept like the dead. I think there are still sheet marks on the side of my face. I haven't slept like that in an age."

"I wish I could sleep that way. I've been an insomniac for weeks."

"I'm sorry, honey. I know that's frustratin'."

"It's okay. As long as *you're* getting sleep, that's what matters to me."

"Thanks, honey. Can I help with dinner?"

"Absolutely not. You sit and relax. In fact, why don't I pour you a glass of something cold, and you can rest some more while I finish up here?"

"You're spoiling me." Rita chortled. "But I won't object."

"One more thing . . ." Julie replied, glancing at Rita out of the corner of her eye.

"Yes?"

Julie inhaled a sharp breath. "I want you to know that I realise this is crazy. So, let's just get that out in the open right now."

"Hmmm… that's a promisin' start," Rita quipped with a wink.

"You recall I went to dinner with James?"

"How could I forget? My wonderful doctor. Handsome, too."

Julie blushed. "He is, both of those things. Anyway, he's invited me to go to Australia with him next week on a business trip, and I agreed."

Rita gaped. For a moment she couldn't formulate a sentence, which was very unlike her. "Australia? Next week?"

"He has a spare ticket. Someone cancelled at the last moment. And on impulse, he asked me to go with him. You know I want to meet my family there… I wasn't expectin' I'd get to do that anytime soon given the state of my life, so this seemed like an opportunity that was too good to miss."

"Your life is fine, honey," Rita stated resolutely. "You'll get through all this and come out the other side, I promise you that."

"I'm glad you're confident, but I'm not sure… I don't know if I can pull myself together enough to finish my doctorate."

"Of course you can. You need a break, and there's nothing to be ashamed of in that. Every one of us needs a break sometime. You're the first in our family to go to college—did you know that? My kids didn't go, but you did. And we're all so proud of you."

Julie sighed. "I know it. There's a lot of pressure."

"It's a privilege. And one you deserve. If you want to go to Australia, I'm not going to stand in your way. I do think it's kind of wild, to be honest. You barely know him."

"I've known him since we were kids."

"But he's a different person now. You don't *really* know him. You think you do, but he could be someone completely different to who we've seen at the hospital."

"I don't think so. He seems genuine to me. And besides, I'll have my own hotel room if I need some space — it's already booked and paid for."

Rita's frown faded into a tentative smile. "Well then, honey, I hope you have a great time together."

After dinner, Rita needed some time to think. She hadn't mentioned the trip to Julie again, but it'd been on her mind. Should she step in? Is that what Helen would've wanted? She didn't think so. Helen was so like their own mother—she would've given Julie the information she thought she needed to make a decision and then would've left her to it. Rita hoped she was doing it the right way. It was so hard to be an aunt sometimes, without the authority to be a mother, but with no one else there to fill the job. She often felt the urge to intervene but held herself back. Maybe she was wrong.

With a shrug, she wandered to her bedroom and took out the box of letters and photographs she'd stowed under her bed to continue reading. She'd been too tired lately to even consider looking them over. But she felt a little better after her nap and was curious to see if she could find out anything more about her parents.

The first envelope she pulled from the pile was aged and had a stain on one corner as though a cup of coffee had once sat there. It was sent from her aunt Bedelia in Ojai, California, and addressed to her father, Raymond Lambert. She opened it gingerly and extracted the thin sheets of paper.

Dearest Ray,

It's been too long. I do hope you'll all manage to visit over Christmas this year, although I know the café makes it hard for you to get away. And I'm not going to be able to travel with the new baby, so we may miss each other a little longer.

I was happy to receive your letter last week, telling me all about Rita and Helen and what they've each been up to. I love that Rita plays the piano. I used to do that myself, although not as well as Sylvia. And Helen is enjoying softball? She must have more coordination than I do!

I'm sorry to hear that you and Sylvia have been arguing more. It's strange how memories work, but when I received your letter, for the first time I recalled our parents doing the same for a few years when we were around the age that your girls are. Maybe it's the strain of parenting. But I'm hopeful that the two of you will make it through to the other side and will be praying for you.

I wish I could be there, but unfortunately Chris's job keeps us up here away from you all for now. I've been begging him to look for work back home in Atlanta, but so far he says he's happy where he is. And so, I'm stuck far away from everyone I love.

It's not all bad though, of course. The town here is lovely, and the people are welcoming, although I'm never going to be accepted as a local. They have a very established social order, and I'm not part of it. Still, I love my little ones, and I'm grateful I can spend each day with them.

Write again soon. Or better yet, come and visit when you can.

With love from your sister,
Bedelia

Rita put the letter away and returned the envelope to its place in the box. Her brow furrowed. Her father hadn't been the letter-writing type, so she was surprised that he'd written to his sister. Not to mention the fact that he'd confided in her about his marriage. She couldn't picture her father doing that, but then again, he and his sister had always been close throughout their lives.

She chose the next letter from the bunch and tugged it free of the envelope. It was sent by her mother around six months later, but originated from her grandparents' address in Rodanthe, North Carolina. After Aunt Penny, her mother's sister, had lived there several years, her folks moved up there to live close by in their twilight years. Penny had never gotten the chance to return to Atlanta and stayed in North Carolina until the day she died. But at least she'd had her parents with her for a while. Then her children kept her there, since they were well established by that point. Rita wondered if she ever regretted that, or came to peace with her new home at some stage. She hoped she found peace, although she'd never asked the question while her aunt was alive. There were so many things she wished she'd been more curious about earlier in life.

Ray,

I hope things are going well for you at home. We're settled in with Mom and Dad now after a few days here. It took Helen a little while to adjust with her nap schedule —you know how she is. Although I don't know how much longer she'll take an afternoon nap, she fights it so often.

Otherwise, she's fine and is loving the trips to the beach with her pail and shovel. She gets sand all over her, in every single crevice. But she doesn't mind one little bit. She could easily live at the beach. Her hair is wild and knotted, her knees are grazed from the number of times she's fallen, and her nose and cheeks are red from the sun and wind. But she's having the time of her life.

Rita is more subdued. I think she knows there's something going on between you and me. She heard us arguing, and she's asked me a few times if we're fighting and when we'll be going home. I tell her we're just here for a vacation, but I'm not sure she believes me.

It is true, though. I need a vacation. You know that. I've been run off my feet for years, with the two girls and the business. It's a lot for anyone to handle, and with my asthma, it only makes things harder. I hope you can understand that I needed to get away.

Not only because I'm tired, but because of the things you said. I don't know how to process it. I've made mistakes, Ray, but so have you. This isn't one person's fault. We can share that blame, without a doubt. But do we need to participate in the blame game? I don't know anymore. I don't know anything at all. I'm completely lost. It scares me at times. I wonder if I'll ever be able to recover. But then I look at the girls' faces and I know that I have to try. For their sakes.

You have to speak to Bill. He's your brother. You own a business together. You can't let things lie. I know that's what you prefer to do, but the two of you have got to work things out between you. You owe it to the café at the very least. You've built something special together, and you can't let it sink because of a dispute.

I don't know how long we'll be here. I only know I have to stay until I can face things again. Will that ever happen? I can't say. I feel weak now, and I need to become stronger. The fighting and yelling was too much for me. The anger was never-ending. I can't live that way. And you shouldn't want to either.

Even in the midst of it all, I wish you the best and send my love.

Your Sylvia

Rita put the letter away with the others and leaned back on her bed, one arm beneath her head. She stared at the ceiling, thinking about what she'd read. It had shaken her more than she'd expected. She remembered the trip to her grandparents' place. They'd bought a small townhouse close to Aunt Penny's near the beach. They'd moved there when Rita was around six or seven years old.

She couldn't quite recall all of the details of their visits to see their grandparents, but there were flashes of memories. Helen in her little terrycloth shorts, with her pail in hand, laughing as the waves lapped at her feet. The water was cold, and it had shocked Rita at first. But gradually she'd learned to love it. They must've been there a while that time, although she couldn't be sure how long. She recalled celebrating her eighth birthday there though, it'd been such fun but she'd missed seeing her Dad.

She'd forgotten all about the fighting between her folks. But now that she read the letter, she recalled feeling scared and upset on the drive north. It must've been due to the tension between her parents. Reading between the lines, it seemed as though her father was fighting with everyone in his life. What could've caused that? Why was he so angry? And why had her mother felt the only option she had was to take her daughters away?

Her memories of her father during her childhood years were good ones. Yes, he was the grouchy type, but she never took it to heart. He loved her—she knew that. And he was a good man, albeit a short-tempered one. He didn't speak often, but when he did, he meant it. She'd always appreciated that about him. So, what were they yelling at each other about? Was it the common issue of financial pressures, raising children, growing a business? Or was there something more to it? Something she still knew nothing about after all these years?

Chapter Thirteen

A week after her customer handed over a napkin with a hastily scrawled name and number on it, Matilda stood in the middle of a busy veterinarian's office wearing a business suit and heels. She wobbled in her heels, her heart racing. Sweat formed beneath her armpits, and she wished she could turn right back around and run outside. But she'd made this appointment to visit the office and look it over, and she couldn't back out now.

"Can I help you?" a perky receptionist asked.

She nodded. "I'm here to see Todd Wheatley. My name is Matilda Berry-Merritt."

"Thank you, Matilda. I'll let him know you're here. Please take a seat."

She sat on a row of plastic chairs between a woman holding a shaking Chihuahua and a man with a cat that kept hissing through the wire door of his carrier.

"He's a gentle guy, really," the man said apologetically. "He doesn't like coming to the vet's office, that's all."

"Not unusual," Matilda replied, her voice croaky.

She always lost her voice when she was stressed, and the

sight of this packed office made her anxious. She was excited too, but anxiety was winning at the moment. If she bought this place, it would be a huge investment. A burden for her to carry. She couldn't move, or take a vacation, or really do anything she wanted to on the spur of the moment. She'd be committed. Tied down. She'd never really felt that way before, and she wasn't sure if she wanted it.

She'd already filed the paperwork for her registration to sit the examination that would allow her to practice in the USA. With Ryan's help, she had the down payment she needed to purchase the business. Looking around, she could see that it needed some renovations. It'd clearly been years since anything had been updated. The walls could use some paint. The furnishings were old. The layout of the waiting room was poky and crowded. If she bought it, she'd want to make some changes. But could she handle that much responsibility?

A man in a long white coat walked through a doorway. He looked to be in his sixties, and his head was balding on top. He wore glasses and peered around the room, clearly looking for someone. She raised a hand.

"Ms Berry-Merritt?" he asked.

She nodded and stood. "You must be Mr Wheatley. Pleased to meet you."

He shook her hand and smiled. "Come with me. I'll show you around the place."

She followed him through a door and into a long hallway. There were small rooms off the hallway. Some doors were open, and some were shut.

"These are our treatment rooms. There are five vet techs working today. They do most of the prep, and then I see the animal once everything else is done. That way, I can spend about five minutes with each animal. I can move from room to room, and it keeps things flowing."

"That's an efficient setup," Matilda said.

"It works pretty well, although as you can see, the whole place needs a facelift." He stopped and pushed a door open. "Here's one of the treatment rooms. There's no one in here right now."

By the time the tour was over, she had a good feel for the place. They finished in his office. He sat behind a messy desk and crossed one leg over the other. She perched opposite him in a hard chair that wobbled.

"I have a loyal base who bring their pets to me regularly. I want my customers to have a good experience and for their animals to be taken care of consistently, so I'd prefer to sell the whole business as one entity rather than selling off the pieces bit by bit."

"That makes sense."

"What do you think of the place?" he asked.

She smiled. "I think you've built something really special here. It's busy, but it doesn't feel cold. Like you care about your patients, and that's really important to me."

"I do care about them. It's the reason I went into the business all those years ago, although it's hard to remember that sometimes, with all the spreadsheets and time cards. But I've loved most of it."

"I suppose my main concern is that I've never run a business before. I worked as a vet in Australia, but I was on staff. I wasn't managing the place. And I'm not sure if I'm up for it."

He leaned forward in his chair, eyes sparkling. "Your honesty is refreshing, which makes me believe you'll do just fine. I'm looking for someone who cares, who'll put their heart and soul into looking after my customers and their pets. I've worked so hard to build this place, I want it to last. If you buy the business, my accountant can help you manage it—he's already agreed to that. And I'm going to be sticking around close by for a while, so you can call me with any questions you have. But as I said, as long as you care, the rest will be fine. It works like a well-oiled machine right now, so you can simply step in and take over."

"I'd want to renovate," she replied. "So, I'd have to close the place down for a little while."

"I figured as much. And if I was sticking around, I'd do the same. Which is fine—people will understand. Just make sure you communicate with the mailing list regularly and let them know what's going on. I don't think it'll be an issue."

After Matilda left, she drove to meet Ryan at the Honeysuckle Café. She wasn't rostered on a shift, but they'd agreed to have lunch together, and she wanted to try out the new buffalo buttermilk chicken burger with thick-cut fries. It looked delicious and made her mouth water every time she served it to someone. After all, it was important for her to be able to describe each dish to the customers. At least, that was her excuse for trying everything.

They sat at a table in the front near the window and ordered quickly, since Ryan had to get back to work.

"I'm starving," he said, tapping his fingers on the tabletop.

She agreed. "I was so nervous about my meeting, I missed breakfast."

"How did it go?"

"It was great. I really like the place and what he's done with it. It needs work. But I don't think it'll be overwhelming. I'll defer to your judgement on that, though."

"You want me to take a look?"

"Yes, please. I need your expert opinion. I think the building is sound, but I'd love your input. After all, you're helping me with the deposit."

"I'm glad to do it," he replied as the waiter brought their burgers and fries. He immediately put one in his mouth. "Ugh. Hot."

She couldn't help laughing. "Maybe slow down, then."

"Can't. I'll die of starvation."

"Do you think I should do it?"

"Do what?"

"Buy the business. It's a huge commitment. It'd tie me down. And I have no idea what I'm doing, so it'll take up a lot of my time trying to figure everything out. It's very profitable for him right now, so I'm hopeful that will continue if I take over. Although, we are likely to lose some customers simply because of the change."

"That makes sense, but it still sounds like it'd be a fantastic opportunity."

"It's a lot of money..." she muttered.

He shrugged. "It's an investment."

"True, but can we manage it?"

"We can manage. I'll get my accountant to look over the books just to make sure everything's as it should be."

"And I've got some people to call to follow up on references."

"But if it all checks out, I think you should go for it, if that's what you want. These kinds of opportunities don't come along every day. It's an established business, ready for you to step into. And it won't come without its challenges, of course, and its commitments, but if this is something that would fulfil you, I fully support you going for it."

"Thanks, sweetie, I appreciate that. It means a lot to me."

"And if you don't enjoy it, or our circumstances change, you can always resell it."

"That's true, I guess. It doesn't have to be a lifelong commitment."

"Not at all. Fix it up, get it going, and if you want to sell it, that's something we can look at."

"But what about Rita? And the café?" She gestured to the room full of customers seated around them.

He nodded. "That's something to consider. How do you feel about telling her?"

"I don't know. She's going through a lot. I'm worried it will make things harder for her."

"Even if you don't buy the business, you weren't planning on staying at the café long term, were you?"

"No, not really. I'm helping her out. That's all."

"And she knows that?"

"We've spoken about it. And she seemed fine with me moving on to other things."

"I'm sure she understands that you can't stay here forever. She'd want you to do what makes you happy."

"I guess I have to decide what that is. Apart from you, of course." She grinned at him.

He reached for her hand and held it gently. "You make me happy as well. So happy."

"I'm glad, because you're stuck with me."

He laughed. "You're stuck with me too. And hopefully, one day we'll have a family."

"I'd love that. I can't believe we've never discussed this, but how many kids do you want?"

"One or two, I guess." He frowned. "I hadn't thought much about it. But I know I definitely want at least one. What about you?"

"Five," she replied.

"Five? That's a lot of children."

"Well, I'll probably scale down that number as soon as I have one. That's what Stella always says. She thinks I'm crazy to want so many. She has three now, and she's done."

"I guess we'll take them as they come."

"And when we do have kids, I want to stay home with them while they're young, so maybe I shouldn't buy this business. Does it even make sense?"

"I say go for it. We can always reevaluate later if we need to. This chance might not come again."

She inhaled a short breath. "Then I think I'm going to do it."

"Awesome! I think you should."

Chapter Fourteen

The dining room at the Honeysuckle Café was buzzing with the usual midmorning coffee seekers—a couple holding hands and laughing together, two friends discussing an issue in muted tones and with serious faces, and a trio from a local business sipping coffee and discussing strategy.

Rita glanced around in satisfaction as she headed for her office. Everything was running smoothly, as it should after so many years. Cathy wasn't making waves today, which was a relief to Rita, who didn't have the energy to deal with it. She seemed to have taken Rita's words to heart after their last discussion.

"Rita!" Amanda called, then jogged towards her.

"Hi. I was going to stop by the kitchen later to say hello. Didn't want to disturb you."

Amanda gave her a hug. "How are you?"

Rita was surprised. Amanda had never been much for displays of affection. "I'm feeling a little better each day."

"You've lost weight." She looked concerned.

Rita nodded. "That happens. I haven't been eating much. But my appetite is back today."

"I'm going to make you something. I'll bring it to the office. I know what you like." Amanda flashed a smile.

"Well, thanks, honey. You're sweet as pie."

"Pie. I'll bring you some of that too."

"I don't deserve you." Rita replied.

In the office, Rita got to work ordering supplies and paying bills. It seemed to be a never-ending task, one she hadn't got around to training anyone else to do. Maybe she could ask one of the staff to help her with it at some stage. Or at least to be a backup for her. She should really ensure someone else was across the books other than herself since she might be out of action even more during the next round of treatment.

She stopped and leaned back in her chair to rub her eyes. She was tired. She might take another nap after lunch. Amanda knocked on the door, then pushed it open. She held a plate with a chicken sandwich and fries on it, along with a pickle spear.

"Thought you might like to try this one. It's new on the menu. Cathy suggested it, and it's been selling like crazy."

"It was Cathy's idea?" Rita took the plate. "I'm glad to hear she's contributin' ideas. Thank you, honey."

"You're welcome." Amanda pressed both hands to her hips. "You let me know if you need anything else."

"Will do. You and Cathy are getting along better, then?"

Amanda exhaled. "She's frayin' my nerves a little less. That's about all I can say for now."

"Well, that's somethin', at least."

After Amanda left, Rita took a bite of the sandwich and let her eyes drift shut in delight. It was delicious—a mixture of salty, spicy and creamy, with a crunchy filet of fried chicken at the centre along with a tart and creamy dressing, crispy lettuce, tomato and pickles.

When she was done, she wiped her hands clean and

pulled a large envelope out of her purse. She'd stowed some of the correspondence she'd found in the box at home in the larger envelope so she could read it today at the office. She was dying of curiosity, wondering if there'd be any further clues in the letters about her parents' marriage or the conflict at the café. She knew her father and his brother had a falling out all those years ago, but she hadn't learned the truth of what happened. What if these letters had nothing else of interest in them? She might never learn the truth about the past, and she'd have to come to terms with that. There was no way for the dead to speak, but letters they'd written could help.

The next letter she read was from her grandmother to her father. Rita's paternal grandmother had been a quiet and reserved woman. Rita didn't recall her speaking much, but when she did, she used a steady, gentle voice, and people listened. Rita's father certainly did.

Darling Ray,

Daddy and I are enjoying California. I never thought we'd get to visit, and now that we're here, I wish we could stay longer. There's so much to see. It's very different from back home. It's dry here, and the wind is warm. There are hills, and some mountains too, although where we are is flat.

We went with your sister and her family to Disneyland yesterday. The kids were over the moon about it. I can't say I blame them. There's everything you could imagine and more for a kid to do. Not to mention the food and the shows! Dad and I had a great time, even if I did avoid the wilder rides. I'm not up for that kind of thing anymore.

I'm sorry you couldn't come visit your sister with us this time. Maybe next time? But I know you have a lot to tend to at home. Have you heard from Sylvia and the girls lately? It makes my heart ache to think of y'all being so far apart. And three months is too long for a family to be separated. I know y'all love each other. You need to do everything you can to work things out.

And on the subject of reconciliation, you've got more than one to make. Don't forget your brother, my boy. The two of you have been as close as peas in a pod your whole lives, and you can't let anything come between you. It's over, and you've both got lives to live. Let the past stay in the past.

You both fell in love with the same woman. There's no crime in that. But to let that come between blood brothers—that's for certain a crime, at least in my eyes. Blood matters more than any other tie. And you've got to understand that your brother is a proud man, just as you are. If you don't make the first move towards reconciliation, he might not either, and then you'll have this rift between you forever.

That's enough of a lecture from me. I only wrote to let you know how we're doing, and that we'll be back as planned on the fifth. No need to pick us up from the airport—we'll get a taxi. I know you have your hands full with the business. I'm not sure how you're managing on your own, but you were always more than capable.

All my love,
Momma

Rita stared at the letter for a long time before folding it away. What was Grandma Beatrice talking about? Dad and Uncle Bill were in love with the same woman? When was that? Who was that? And why would that cause them to fight so many years later when each of them had married someone else?

Three months in North Carolina—that's what the letter said. Three months of family separation. And maybe it lasted even longer. It must've been so difficult for her father to be alone, to manage the café without his partner and his wife. They'd previously all worked there together. The abrupt change must've pushed him to his limits. How had he coped?

There was a knock at the office door.

"Come in!" Rita called.

Cathy opened the door and stepped over the threshold. "I hope I'm not disturbing you." She held a plate of pie aloft, along with a glass of what looked like iced coffee. "I brought dessert."

"Well, aren't you the sweetest thing? You're not interrupting, not at all. I was finishing up some bills." Rita shoved the letter back into the larger envelope and put the lot in her purse under the desk. "How are you today?"

Cathy placed the dessert on Rita's desk and sat in the chair opposite Rita, smoothing the apron she was wearing over her dress. Her blonde hair was teased and styled in waves away from her face that didn't move. Her eyeshadow was blue, and there was thick black eyeliner that swept up at the corner of each eye.

"I'm holdin' on. And you?"

"Doing okay. Sounds like things are workin' out at the café."

"They're fine. I'm just... well, I'll be honest, I'm strugglin'." Tears formed in Cathy's eyes, and she dabbed at them with the tip of a manicured finger.

"Oh, honey. What's wrong?"

Cathy sniffled, searching for a tissue in her sleeve. "It's Gareth. He says he's not going to give me a dime of the house equity. He's selling it right out from under me. I'll have nowhere to go. I'll be homeless!" She burst into tears and smothered her cries in her uncooperative sleeve.

With a sigh, Rita got to her feet and lumbered around the desk to pat her cousin on the back. "I'm so sorry, honey. That's hard."

"And the kids blame me. They say it's all my fault he left. That I'm too mean, and I nitpick him. They think I'm critical and judgemental, and that's what drove him away. But I know he's just feedin' all that to them. They can't seem to locate an independent thought to save their lives."

"That happens sometimes. It's hard for kids to understand these things even when they're grown."

"I know it. But he's lying to them. He left me because he's found someone else. He just won't admit it—not to me or to them. But I've got the evidence, and I know who she is. I can't tell the kids, though. They love that man. Heaven knows why. But they do."

"Well, he's their daddy."

"I know it. They don't want to think badly of him, and I don't want them to either. But I'm going to end up homeless and alone if he gets his way. No place to lay my head, and my grown kids, who I dedicated my life and heart to raisin', wanting nothing to do with me. I can't see a way out of this."

"They'll come around. And as far as the house is concerned, he can't toss you out of your own place. You stay put. The law will have your back on that one."

"Are you sure?"

"Is it in your name?"

"It's in both names. But he says since he made the payments all those years while I stayed home with the kids, the law will side with him and say it's his."

"I can't believe that's true," Rita replied with a shake of her head. "He's trying to manipulate you. The law says that the house belongs to the two of you. And if it's sold, you'll both have to agree and you'll get an equal share. Have you got yourself a lawyer yet?"

"I've found one, but I haven't signed the paperwork yet. It's a lot of money, and I don't know if I'm going to be able to afford a thing. I'll be penniless. At least that's what Gareth says. That I've leeched off him long enough and he's cutting me loose."

"Leeched?" Rita saw red. "Well, I'll be darned…"

"I'm sorry," Cathy said. "I'm bawling all over your office."

"No, you're not, and you're fine. There've been plenty of tears shed in this room over the years—don't you worry about that. Now, listen up. You didn't leech off anyone. You had a partnership with this man. The two of you agreed that he would earn, and you'd raise the family. It's an equal partnership. And that means any resources built by the family over the course of your marriage are communal property."

Cathy blinked. "Is that true?"

"That's the way I see it. I don't know the exact legal terminology, but I do know the law tries to be fair. They're not going to leave you homeless and without a nickel to your name."

"So, I should stay in the house?"

"Don't you move out until you're ready to or want to. No matter what he says. That's your home. If he chose to leave because he wants to be with someone else, that's on him. And if you need to take some time off from the café to manage all of this, you let me know."

Cathy shook her head. "No, I love coming here. It distracts me. And I can be myself here. No one knows anythin' about what I'm goin' through and I like it that way."

"Well, whatever works for you. I'm here and I'll do what I can to help. I hope you know that."

"I know you are. And I'm grateful," Cathy replied. "I'm sorry I've been such a witch."

Rita laughed. "Haven't we all, Cathy? There's a season for everything, and this is the season of Cathy startin' over. You have a fresh slate. Nothing written on it yet. Life can be anything you want it to be."

Cathy huffed. "I don't know how you stay so positive, Rita. The world throws you a rotten lemon, and somehow you turn it into lemonade."

Rita bent to give her a hug. "Well, who wants to suck on a rotten lemon? Not me. Lemonade tastes so much sweeter."

Chapter Fifteen

The day finally arrived. Julie was going to Australia. Her bags were packed and sitting by the front door. Blue stood guard over them. She'd showered and was dressed, making herself a cup of coffee in the kitchen when she heard the car pull into the drive.

She took a few sips of the scalding-hot drink, then poured the rest down the sink, her stomach flip-flopping with nerves. She checked her fanny pack again for her passport, tickets, lip balm, hand sanitiser and a few other odds and ends. It was all there.

Then she went to open the door. James was there, one hand poised to knock. Blue wagged his tail at James. He wasn't much of a guard dog. James wore Dockers and a blue collared shirt. He smelled as though he was fresh from the shower.

"Ready to go?" he asked.

She nodded.

He grabbed her large bag while she took the carry-on and her purse. Then she followed him out to the black town car. The driver helped them with the luggage, and the two of them sat in the back seat while he finished up.

"I can't believe I'm going overseas today. I've never been overseas before," Julie said.

James arched an eyebrow. "Never?"

"Nope. I had a passport because I almost went to Haiti with a group from church last year, but the trip was cancelled."

"Well, I consider it an honour that your first time is with me." He laughed.

She blushed. "I'm glad I'm with you, actually, because at least I have someone to help me not do something truly stupid like... fall off the jet bridge."

"That definitely would be stupid. But I don't think that's likely."

"I'm so nervous. I feel like I'm going to burst out of my skin."

He smiled. "This car just happens to come equipped with champagne. Would you like some?"

"Champagne? That would be perfect right now. It's after five o'clock, right?"

"Even later in LA. That's good enough for me."

There was a bottle in a cooler between them. James popped the bottle open and poured them each a glass. It bubbled up to the top but didn't spill over.

He held his aloft. "Here's to our adventure together."

She smiled and clinked her glass to his. "To our adventure."

They drank and chatted excitedly about the trip all the way to the airport. Traffic was heavy, so it was nice that neither one of them had to worry about driving. And they had plenty of time to get there. Julie's nerves gradually dissipated until she was completely relaxed by the time they arrived.

The driver unloaded their luggage, and they wheeled it inside to check in. James was very helpful, walking her through every step. The truth was, she'd never flown anywhere. It was hard to admit at twenty-five years of age, but there it was. She'd only ever driven to neighbouring states and had never gone far enough from home to need to take a flight there. The process was starting to make her heart hammer again.

When they reached the gate, she sat down with a sigh of relief. "I can't believe we actually made it on time. I thought we'd never get through that line at security."

"It can take a while," James agreed. "But we still have a little over an hour until boarding. Would you like to get a drink?"

"Yes, if we have time."

"It's after five here now."

She laughed. "Perfect. Maybe we should grab something to eat as well."

"They'll serve us dinner on the plane, but we could get a little snack if you like."

"I'd love something. I was too nervous to eat lunch."

They found a small restaurant with a cozy English pub feel to it and sat at a booth in the back. Then they ordered an appetiser platter to share and a cider each.

"Do you remember when we found your mother's home-made blackberry wine that Christmas when I stayed with you?" James asked as soon as the waiter left them.

Julie laughed. "I'd forgotten all about that. Yes! That's right. The blackberry wine. She said it helped soothe her stomach. She used to get stomach aches all the time. If only she'd gone to the doctor, instead she learned how to make blackberry wine from Grandma."

James nodded. "That was the first time I was ever drunk in my life."

"I hope so. You were only fifteen."

"And you were only twelve."

"I know. I can't believe I got drunk on wine with you at twelve. That's terrible!"

"I was a bad influence, clearly."

"I don't think we knew it would make us drunk, though. Did we?"

"Oh, I definitely knew." He winked at her. "I was a little bit curious what you'd be like with some wine. Of course, looking back now, I realise how bad that was. I should apologise... I hope you haven't become an alcoholic or something."

"I *knew* it was your fault!"

He laughed. "Definitely my fault. But I also have to admit that I kind of had fun with you that day. It was the first time I really felt like maybe we were friends, and that you didn't hate me."

"Hate you?"

"Yeah, you seemed pretty put out that I came to stay at first. I wasn't sure how to get through to you. But the wine seemed to do the trick."

"I definitely didn't hate you, but I was probably a bit peeved that Mom was giving you all of her attention. Before you came along, it was just me and her. We were a team. Us against the world. And the world threw a lot at us, let me tell you."

"I can understand that."

Their food arrived at the table, along with the ciders. Julie took a big swig of hers. It was sweet and tart, perfect for how she was feeling. She ate a couple of fries dipped in garlic aioli.

"Over time, I grew to like you," she said.

"I'm glad to hear it. I liked you a lot. Both of you. Although it was a hard time for me, being away from my parents and dealing with the divorce."

"I'm sure it was. I realise that now. Of course, at the time I wasn't thinking about that. I was focused on how you were horning in on my territory." She chuckled. "It's funny how selfish kids can be, huh?"

"Absolutely. But you weren't too bad."

"High praise!" She laughed.

He shrugged. "It's about all a fifteen-year-old boy can say about a twelve-year-old girl. Honestly, you were kind of annoying at times. But you could be a lot of fun too, and by the time I left there, I knew you were someone I could trust forever. Even now, I feel like I know who you are and that you're the kind of person I could rely on just because of that time we spent together. It's a strange kind of connection, but a real one."

"I know what you mean. I feel it too. Like you're steady, true, reliable. I trust you deep down, even though I don't really know you. Or I haven't known you in a long time."

He nodded, eyes sparkling. "It's nice. I don't have any siblings. Or close friends. I've been so busy in recent years, studying, working... I haven't focused on building those relationships. I have my friends at work. But we don't hang out much after work."

"I can understand that. I didn't become a fancy doctor like you . . ." She nudged him beneath the table with her foot. "But I've been so focused on my studies that I can't think of many people who'd miss me much now that I'm gone. My ex-boyfriend probably noticed that I'm not there any longer. And maybe the girl who lived next door to my dorm room. My supervisor, of course, and perhaps some of the other PhD candidates. But most of my good friends left after graduation and kind of drifted out of my life."

"It's nice to have someone to talk to," he agreed.

"Definitely."

Before long, they finished up and wandered back to the gate just in time to board. Their tickets were business class, so they were some of the first on board. Julie was feeling a little buzzed and was beyond excited that her first time travelling was business class. The chairs were enormous, with their own television screen and a bunch of other features in the armrest that she immediately started checking out. James' seat was right next to hers. The stewardess brought them each another glass of champagne while they waited for the rest of the passengers to board.

James handed her a couple of aspirin. "You should take these and have a glass of water. It's good to drink throughout the flight, you can easily get dehydrated otherwise."

She nodded. "Thanks. Good idea."

He took some as well. Then they settled in for their journey. Julie couldn't wait to get there. She was happy to be travelling with James and having this adventure, but in the back of her mind, she was constantly aware that she might meet her sister and brothers for the very first time. She only hoped they'd be as happy to see her as she was to see them. She hadn't told them she was coming. It felt too real, too scary, to set anything up. And she might change her mind the moment the flight landed. But if she missed this opportunity, she might never get another one. And the thought made her head spin.

Chapter Sixteen

Life was changing for Matilda. She'd decided to purchase the veterinary business. Her anxiety levels were up and down, but she mostly felt pretty good about the choice. And Ryan backed her, which meant the world to her. All she needed to do now was get Rita's blessing. She still hadn't been able to bring herself to talk to Rita about it, but she planned on getting to the café early for her meeting with Todd. They were having coffee together with his lawyer so she could sign the paperwork. Ryan's lawyer had already looked over it and she'd gotten approval for a business loan at the bank, of course with Ryan's backing — since she didn't make nearly enough money at the café to land a loan of that size.

She couldn't get over how supportive her new husband was. Every day she spent with him convinced her more and more that she'd made the right choice by marrying him. They'd fallen in love so quickly, her sister Stella had worried that she didn't know him well enough. But ever since, her love for him had only grown stronger and deeper.

At the café, she parked her car. It was raining hard, with heavy drops thundering on the roof. She searched the back seat for an umbrella, and pulled it out from the foot well. Then she rushed to the café door with rain splashing in at her from every side.

She shook the umbrella dry in the entry and placed it in the stand. Then she glanced around the café while she fixed her hair. It was early. There were a few regulars at the tables and a small line at the counter, but it wasn't too busy. No sign of Rita—she was most likely in her office or out in the courtyard. She often liked to sit out there when it rained to watch the water drop down the honeysuckle plant and into the other potted plants that were scattered around the space.

That was where she found her, seated on a chair with a smile on her face.

"Matilda, take in that glorious scent. I love the smell of rain on honeysuckle."

"It's getting a lovely drink today." Matilda sat next to her and leaned over to kiss her on the cheek. "You're looking well."

"Thanks, honey. I'm feeling much better today."

"Glad to hear it. I hate when you're low."

"Not a fan of it myself. And I appreciate your concern. What can I do for you, honey?" Rita turned to face her.

Matilda wiped a raindrop from her cheek. "I need to talk to you about something."

* * *

After she'd spoken to Rita, Matilda relaxed. Her cheeks had been flushed and her heart rate was up, since she'd found the conversation stressful. But now that it was over, the stress had abated, and she was happy to go back inside to sign the necessary paperwork to get things going.

Rita had been happy for her. Not in a polite way, but actually delighted for her. She'd urged Matilda to follow her heart and thanked her for all of the hard work she'd done at the café.

"Cathy has really taken up the slack here lately, honey. You don't have to worry one little bit about leaving us now. You've helped us get through the hardest part. I can't tell you how much I appreciate it."

"I'm glad to be able to do what I can."

Matilda selected a table by the wall that had three chairs. Then she sat with a coffee to wait for Todd and his lawyer. They were early and shook her hand before sitting. Todd looked much more casual than he had the last time she saw him, wearing a pair of jeans and a T-shirt. He was relaxed and happy, which she was glad to see. She knew how much the business meant to him and was excited to take it on, knowing it would help him realise his retirement dreams.

The lawyer, Mike Bunting, was a man with a mostly bald head and a pair of black-rimmed spectacles. His suit was immaculate, and he barely spoke throughout the meeting. Which Todd more than made up for—she hadn't met anyone as chatty as Todd in her entire life. But she enjoyed his constant monologue. It helped fill the silence as she read over the contract.

"You've had the building and pest inspection done?" Mike asked as she scanned that part of the contract.

"That's right," Matilda said.

"Then initial here, please."

She did as he asked.

"And you acknowledge the cooling off period here..." He pointed to the contract, and she signed.

Before long, they were done, and the veterinary clinic was all hers. She couldn't quite believe it. It felt as though the air had been sucked from her lungs — she was terrified but also excited.

The three of them stood and once again shook hands.

"Congratulations, Ms Merritt," Todd said with a smile. "I hope you're as happy working there as I have been."

"I'm sure I will be. And thank you so much. You've been so helpful throughout this whole process."

"You're very welcome."

The two men left and Matilda packed up her things slowly, trying hard to process what had just happened. Her life had changed in the course of a single morning. She'd resigned from her position at the café and had purchased a large and busy enterprise. She only hoped she hadn't made an enormous mistake.

Back at home, Ryan was waiting for her with a bottle of champagne. He popped the bottle the moment she emerged up the stairs, then poured it into two glasses and handed her one. He kissed her on the lips and wrapped his free arm around her waist to pull her close.

"Congratulations, baby. I'm so proud of you."

She smiled and took a sip of the champagne. "Thanks, love. Couldn't have done it without you. Now the hard work begins."

Chapter Seventeen

Rita could picture them both. Standing there on the dock, poles in hand. Uncle Bill smoked and Dad would wave the smoke away with a manufactured cough, glaring at his brother if it drifted too close. Then Bill would remove the cigarette from his mouth and beam at Dad until Dad shook his head and went back to fishing.

They were close. Two brothers, only a couple of years apart. They looked nothing alike, but they shared the same laugh. She could remember it all like it was yesterday. It was such a shame what'd happened between them. That something could've driven them so far apart until they died still mired in the pain and conflict. It tore at her heartstrings.

She pulled the truck into the café parking lot and climbed out, half expecting her bones to creak. Gradually she was getting back into driving herself around and living her life again after weeks of treatments. Soon, she'd be back in that chair again. But until then, she intended to do as much as she could to keep the business going.

Inside, she found Cathy seated in the dining area, looking over receipts. There was always a lull at this time of the morning, and the entire place was empty. It wouldn't be long before the lunch crowd began to filter in, though. Rita sat beside Cathy with a sigh.

"How are you, Cathy?"

Cathy's brow was furrowed in concentration. "Fine. You?"

"I'm holding it together most days. Which is an achievement in itself."

"You can say that again." Cathy gave her a wan smile. "I'm looking for a lost receipt. I want to make sure we have everything in order for the books. Any ideas?"

"Could've fallen to the floor and then got kicked under the desk. It happens sometimes."

"I'll take a look there. Thanks."

"You're welcome. Hey, I've been meaning to talk to you about something. I found a few of my parents' things locked away in a storage closet at the lake house."

"Really? Wow. That's been there a while, then."

"I knew the closet was full of their stuff, but I've been avoiding it for years. I thought since I was having some time off, it would be good to go through it and get rid of anything I don't want to keep. And I stumbled across this box of letters."

"Letters? From who?"

"Different people who wrote to Mom and Dad over the years. And there's mention of your dad in there—the issues he had with mine. I'm hoping one of the letters will tell me details because I still don't understand why they'd give up on each other the way they did."

Cathy nodded slowly, her face somber. "I know that it was some kind of betrayal. That's what Dad used to talk about. He said he came up with the idea for the café and even named it. He was the one who signed the original lease. And he asked Uncle Ray to join him, since Ray was flailing a bit with a young family and no career prospects. He was so happy when Uncle Ray joined him and said it gave him the confidence to make it happen. Ray had such great ideas about the menu and how to run things. I still remember when he came up with the recipe for their famous gumbo."

"We use that recipe every day," Rita agreed.

"It's a great recipe. But we were all devastated when Dad walked away from the business he started. And from his brother. They were such great friends."

"You don't have any idea why? What happened? One of the letters I read seemed to suggest it had something to do with love. That maybe they fought over a woman years earlier. But why didn't the rift happen then? Why wait so long to get angry? Something must've triggered it."

Cathy shrugged. "That's all news to me. I guess love makes sense. Otherwise, why would they be so secretive about the whole thing?"

"And why would the conflict last for so long? Love is definitely the most logical explanation."

"I wonder who she was."

"We may never know. But I've brought some of the letters with me to the office. I read them in between administrative tasks. I'm so curious about what happened. And I thought you should know about it, since it impacts you."

"Thanks for telling me. I appreciate it. And keep me updated if you discover anything new."

"I will."

Cathy hesitated. "I've held that against you for a long time, you know."

"What?" Rita frowned.

"That it was my father who came up with the idea and named the business. I've always felt as though this place was my heritage and that you stole it from me."

Rita was about to argue when Cathy waved her off.

"Don't worry—I don't feel that way anymore. What happened isn't your fault. And you've done such a great job of managing the café. I was insecure and angry. Upset about the conflict between our families and the fact that Dad's legacy was forgotten the way it was. He ended his life working as a plumber and was never as happy again. He loved this café. It was everything to him. His dream come to life."

"Well, I guess I can understand that." Rita pursed her lips. "I'm sorry it happened that way. It seems like such a pointless battle. And I'm angry with both of them for not dealing with it before they passed. They were both so unbelievably stubborn."

Cathy chuckled. "Ain't that the truth."

Chapter Eighteen

When they landed on the Gold Coast in Australia, it was early morning on a Thursday. They'd left at night on Tuesday, which meant that Julie had skipped an entire day. She'd never get to live through that day. It was a strange realisation.

When they landed, the weather was cool, but not cold. It was winter in Australia, but the sun shone in a brand-new day. It was already high in the sky by seven thirty. The sky was a brilliant blue, and the world looked brighter than she'd ever seen it. There was something very different about this land. Excitement electrified her.

They chatted together in anticipation of their adventure as they gathered their luggage from baggage claim and carried it through the very small customs section. From the gate to the exit was a brief walk, and before they knew it, they were standing out in the sunshine, waiting for a taxi.

Everyone around them sounded just like Matilda. Julie immediately loved the accents and found herself smiling uncontrollably.

"What are you grinning about?" James asked her as he pushed sunglasses onto the bridge of his nose.

"I love it here already. I'm supposed to be Australian. I can feel it."

He laughed. "That's a good sign. Did you get any sleep?"

"I slept great. And I watched three different movies. I've never flown before, so I can't say this with certainty, but I don't think I'll ever want to travel in economy."

"I hear you on that," he replied.

It was their turn. A taxi pulled up in front of them, and the driver climbed out. James helped a driver load their luggage into the back of the taxi.

The drive to the hotel was exciting. Julie spent the entire time with the window down, peering out at the sights. The traffic was heavy but didn't slow their progress too much. The air was heating up by the moment, and the sun on her skin felt delicious. They drove close enough to shore that she could see the beach in the distance briefly, and she definitely smelled the salt in the air. She'd only ever seen beaches in Florida and North Carolina, so she was excited to visit them. She hoped they'd have ample time.

They wound past palm trees and neighbourhoods, then into a small city with high-rise buildings, restaurants and packed sidewalks. She wound up her window and smoothed back her windblown hair, grinning at James.

"This is so great," she said.

He smiled. "It's different from what I thought it'd be."

"In the best possible way," she replied with a sigh.

When they reached their hotel, she climbed out of the car and had to strain her neck to see the top of the building. It was very tall. It almost gave her vertigo.

"We're staying here?" she asked.

James nodded. "It's called Q1. The tallest building in Surfer's Paradise."

"I believe it. I only hope we're not too close to the top. I'm not sure I'd be able to stand looking out the window."

She was wrong about that. They were close to the top of the building, and she had no trouble peering out the floor-to-ceiling windows that lined one entire wall. It was an incredible view. She'd had no idea how close they were to the beach. It stretched as far as she could see in both directions. Azure waves curled to shore on brilliantly white sand, so white it was almost blinding from where she stood. Behind the sand were rolling dunes covered in seagrasses and foliage. And before that, a wide footpath with ant-sized people strolling, riding bikes and weaving on skateboards. In either direction, high-rise buildings crowded the shoreline, but quickly petered away into smaller structures.

"This place is called Surfer's Paradise? Where are the surfers?" she asked.

James squinted beside her. "Those black dots might be them."

She saw what he was pointing to. "I think you're right."

"You're okay here?" he asked, scanning the room. "I'm right next door if you need anything. I might go get unpacked and have a shower."

"The room is fantastic." She looked around. There was a king-sized bed, a spacious living area with TV, and a luxurious-looking bathroom. She couldn't wait to get out of her dirty clothing and under a stream of hot water. "I'm tired, but we should try to stay awake until tonight so we're not too jet-lagged."

"I agree. I have to go to the conference tomorrow, so I need to get some sleep tonight."

"We can grab lunch later, if you want," she suggested.

"That sounds good. I'll call you when I'm ready."

"Perfect."

* * *

Two hours later, she was resting in bed. Her eyes were starting to drift shut when the phone rang, startling her into wakefulness.

"Are you ready to go? I fell into the deepest sleep and I'm struggling to wake up, but I'm also starving. Want some lunch?"

She blinked a few times and yawned. "I'm up and almost ready. Give me two minutes."

They found a hibachi restaurant just outside the building. The chef sliced and cooked everything in front of them, even throwing shrimp to James to catch in his mouth. It was delicious and a lot of fun. She hadn't laughed so much in a long time, and James was a good sport about it all.

After lunch, they paid and wandered outside.

"What should we do now?" James asked.

"I really want to see the beach."

He smiled. "Let's go, then."

It wasn't hard to find. They walked a couple of blocks, crossed the street, and there it was, stretching out before them.

Julie had changed into sandals and a sundress with a light cardigan over the top. She slipped her feet out of the sandals and held on to them by the straps, then descended the few stairs to the sand. It was cool on her feet. She squished her toes down into it, joy filling her soul.

"That feel good?" James asked, joining her.

"I love the beach. I hardly ever get to go, and I've never seen one quite like this. It's beautiful."

They set off along the beach without a destination in mind. James reached for her hand as though it was the most natural thing in the world, and they walked that way for half an hour, hand in hand. It was relaxed, and Julie was happy. She had almost forgotten what that felt like.

* * *

Back at the hotel, Julie fought diligently against sleep. She yawned and picked up her Kindle, then got comfortable on the couch with her legs tucked up beneath her. She had a few hours until dinner. They'd both agreed that they'd just try to get through dinner before collapsing in bed. After their long walk on the beach, they were exhausted and had gone back to their respective rooms for a rest and to change for dinner. But she wondered now if they'd given themselves a little too much down time. How on earth would she make it through?

Maybe she should call Stella.

Her heart skipped a beat. The thought of speaking to her biological sister made her breath stick in her throat. She would only be in the country for a week. If she didn't make the phone call soon, she'd run out of time.

She put the Kindle down and picked up her phone. The number was already saved in her address book. Rita got it from Matilda in the hopes that Julie might use it, and now that she was here, it all seemed so much more real. Nervous flutterings in her stomach made her head light.

The phone rang and she stood to pace, unable to sit still any longer.

"Hello. This is Stella."

She hesitated.

"Hello?"

Julie inhaled a quick breath. "Hi, Stella. My name is Julie Brown. I'm your sister."

Chapter Nineteen

The morning started off cool, and Matilda felt autumn on the strong breeze that blew in from the north as she trudged from the car to her new veterinary clinic in the dark. She carried buckets and tools, boxes of supplies and more from the car to the clinic over and over until she was finally done. Ryan would meet her there later. He first had to check in at his construction site and make sure everything was going according to plan there. He had a lot on his plate, and she felt a little guilty adding to it with this renovation. They had so many renovations going on, she'd begun strip paint and sand back surfaces all night long in her dreams.

She set up a speaker and got some inspirational upbeat music playing from the Star 94 radio station. Then she flipped on all of the lights. She'd already had movers come and take out every single piece of furniture. She'd donated all of it rather than wasting money storing it. It was all in bad shape and in desperate need of being replaced. But now that the furniture was gone, the rest of the building looked to be in an even more sad state than she'd remembered.

The walls were a dirty cream colour, with stains and marks

all over them. Paint peeled and was chipped on corners and doorways. The crown moulding had fallen off in places. The carpet was in ruins, even worn through in a few places. And the entire place stank of old socks.

She donned a mask and got to work. The first thing she wanted to do was tear up the carpet. She'd rented a big dumpster, what she call a rubbish skip, and it sat out in the parking lot ready for the reams of carpet and whatever else she found that needed to be thrown out.

For the next three hours, she tore out carpet tacks, and then rolled up strips of carpet one at a time. Then she removed the padding. After what seemed a never-ending series of trips to the dumpster, she'd made her way through half of the waiting room. One piece of carpet was particularly stubborn, and she tugged at it so hard that she flew backwards and landed on her rear end on the concrete floor she'd just cleared.

She cried out in pain just as Ryan walked through the door. He hurried to her, set down the tools he was carrying, and helped her to her feet.

"What happened, darlin'?"

She grimaced. "I fell backwards and landed on my tailbone. I think I might've broken it." She rubbed it gingerly as tears filled her eyes. She blinked them away.

"Aw…" He kissed her cheeks, then wiped the hair from her eyes. "I should've been here."

"You're here now. That's what matters." She nestled into his chest. "It really hurts."

"Maybe you should go to the doctor."

"Let's see if I can walk." She shuffled forwards. There was a sharp pain with each step, but it was bearable. "Ouch. I think I'm okay."

"What do you want to do, then?"

"Let's keep working. We have a lot to finish today if we're going to stay on track with our renovations."

She hesitated, looking around at the trashed room. With a sigh, she reached for his hand. "Am I making a big mistake here?"

He smiled at her. "It's going to be fine. Things always look worse before they get better. Trust me."

It was Friday — Julie had been looking forward to, and dreading, this day since the plane landed on the Gold Coast. She'd arranged to meet her sister and two brothers for dinner nearby at a restaurant she'd plugged into her GPS about fifteen times today already. She was nervous. Actually, that was an understatement. She was terrified. What if they didn't like her? What if they were angry about the revelation that she was their sister? What if they were just truly awful people? She had to admit that Stella seemed likeable enough over the phone, but things could be different in person.

For the past few days, James had attended his conference during the day and Julie had explored the Gold Coast. She'd gone to the beach once. Although it wasn't quite warm enough to swim for long, she had paddled in the water a while and then lay on the sand in the sunshine to warm up again. Thankfully, she still had a bathing suit that fit her, even though she hadn't worn one in months—she couldn't quite remember the last time.

Then she'd gone to SeaWorld for a day. She'd loved the dolphin show and had ridden a number of roller coasters and other rides. She wasn't one for super scary rollercoasters, but she'd done okay. Of course, it wasn't nearly as much fun on your own as it was with someone else, which was too bad. Still, she'd decided to make the most of her trip anyway, and that's what she'd done.

She and James went to the *Outback Spectacular* the previous evening. It'd been her favourite thing so far, with an incredible show of horse riding, acrobatics, tricks and a delicious meal served to them in their seats. Then this morning, she'd strolled through the city and done some shopping—she'd found several lovely outfits, a dress, some pants and a couple of blouses. And everywhere she went, people were very friendly. They'd strike up a conversation out of nowhere, chatting about almost anything. And she lost count of how many said hello or dipped their head in greeting.

There was a knock at her hotel door. She took one last look in the mirror, noting that the beach waves she'd added to her hair suited her. Behind her black-rimmed glasses, her dark eyes were accentuated by a soft brown eyeshadow that complemented her new red dress. She wore a shawl around her shoulders to keep warm. After checking her reflection, she strode to open the door.

"Wow. You look incredible," James said with a whistle.

Her cheeks flamed. "Thank you. You look handsome too." Ever since they'd held hands on the beach, she'd wondered how he felt about her. Did he want more than a friendship? She couldn't tell. Since that day, he'd held her hand a couple more times, but he hadn't done or said anything else that suggested a deeper interest. Even so, they'd had such a great time together over the past few days. She never grew tired of his company. And truly, the more time she spent with him, the more she liked him and wanted to be with him.

"Are you sure you want me to come with you?" he asked. "Because I don't want to make it awkward for you."

"Awkward? I think that ship has already sailed."

He laughed. "I suppose you're right. But I don't want to intrude. This is a private family moment…"

"Please come," she replied. "I don't think I can face it alone."

He nodded. "Right, that does it. I'm coming."

His blond hair was loosely combed, and he wore a pair of blue jeans with a navy knit sweater that fit snugly on his athletic frame. He reached for her hand, and she let him have it before pulling the hotel door shut behind her. She was so grateful to have him with her. It made meeting her family a little less daunting, knowing he was by her side. He was gentle, yet strong, forthright but kind. And she knew that if things went badly tonight, he'd rescue her. He was the rescuing type. No doubt that was why he'd gone into medicine.

They walked down the hallway to the elevator together and she inhaled a deep breath to calm her nerves. This dinner would change her life forever. She was meeting her biological siblings for the first time. She'd always wanted brothers and sisters and now she finally had three. She only hoped she'd make a good impression.

* * *

The restaurant was busy. There was a line of people waiting to put their names down, but Stella had booked ahead. At least, that's what she'd told Julie she'd do, and Julie hoped she had, since otherwise they'd be here all night. Finally, the hostess led them to a table where three adults sat—a woman and two men.

All three looked almost exactly like Julie. So much that it took her breath away.

She stopped still, gaping, then hurried forward on her high

heels to meet them. She felt the immediate urge to cry as Stella pulled her into a strong hug.

"You must be Stella," she said, doing her best to hold it together.

Stella nodded against her shoulder, but didn't respond. She was probably experiencing a similar emotion, since she didn't seem to be able to speak. Then Julie took a step back and noticed that Stella had tears in her red-rimmed eyes, just like Julie did.

Stella dabbed her eyes with a napkin as Julie went around the table. The two men hugged her as well, a little less forcefully than Stella had done, and introduced themselves as Todd and Bryce. Julie still couldn't get past the family resemblance. If she'd had any doubts about where she came from, she didn't any longer. All those years of people teasing her about the way she stood out at family gatherings—them all blonde-haired and blue-eyed, and Julie with her dark hair and eyes, her slightly prominent front teeth, and her fair skin with the smattering of freckles. She knew where she came from now. She belonged to this small group of people looking awkwardly at her around a restaurant table.

She introduced them to James, and then they all sat. It was hard to know what to say. Where to start? There was so much unknown between them. How can one have immediate intimacy with someone they've never met? It would take time, most likely.

"What do you each do for a living?" she asked as they browsed their menus. It was a starting point. Admittedly, not a very creative one, but she had to say something.

"I'm staying home with the kids right now," Stella said. "But usually I'm a solicitor—or lawyer, as you probably call them."

"Oh, right. You have kids? How many?"

"Three of them. And they keep me busy."

"I bet they do."

"I'm a doctor," Todd said with a serious look on his face. "I specialise in paediatrics."

"How wonderful. I bet it's great to work with kids."

He frowned. "It can be."

Bryce laughed, looking far less serious than his brother. "Don't worry—he's always like that. I'm a PE teacher. So, I guess in a way, we all work with children."

Stella laughed. Todd looked annoyed at Bryce's teasing, and Julie nodded empathically. "That's so great. I love kids."

"We're big into kids in this family, so you'll fit right in," Stella replied with a wink. "Mum and Dad were both teachers for part of their careers. Dad went into real estate later, since he said there was no money in teaching, and he couldn't bear to put up with any more of their awful behaviour."

"He was right on both points, unfortunately," Bryce added with a shrug. "But what can you do? I still love it. And what about you, Julie? What do you do?"

"I'm studying psychology. I'm more than halfway through my doctorate, but I've taken a little break at the moment."

"Sometimes a break is exactly what you need," Stella said.

Julie shrugged. "With everything that's happened...I couldn't seem to focus."

Stella, Bryce and Todd exchanged a knowing look.

"I'm sure it's been a shock to you," Todd said in a gentle voice.

Julie felt her throat constrict and tears threaten. She nodded.

"It was a surprise for all of us," Stella said. She reached for Julie's hand and squeezed it. "But a good surprise because we got you out of the deal."

"Thanks for saying that." Julie pushed back the emotion. She looked at James, who dipped his head encouragingly. "Honestly, I've been struggling. Trying to figure out who I am now. My parents…" Her voice broke. "They both died—my dad before I was born, and my mom when I was a teenager. I'd clung on to the idea that they loved me and we were still connected. I know it probably doesn't really matter, but finding out that they weren't my parents…" She couldn't hold the tears back any longer and buried her face in her hands to hide her pain.

Stella's voice was soft. "They *were* your parents. In every way that mattered. Their love for you wouldn't have changed even if they knew. You're still connected to them."

Julie drew a deep breath and pulled herself together. "Do you think they knew?"

"We can't say for sure, but I think so."

"Really?" Julie sniffled into her napkin.

"Dad gave us all DNA test kits for Christmas right before he died. I think he wanted Tilly to find out the truth. Which means, he knew. And if he knew, then your mum probably knew as well."

"But for how long? That's the question," Bryce said, leaning back in his chair. None of them had an answer.

Their food arrived, and for a few minutes, they ate and chatted about their lives. Julie learned that all three of them were very different in personality, even if they looked so similar. The mood lightened, and Julie felt as though a huge burden had been lifted from her shoulders.

Her siblings were fun. Bryce had a great sense of humour. Todd's was dry, and he was mostly very serious. She could see why he made a good doctor. Stella was warm and friendly, full of life and laughter. Julie could imagine the two of them becoming very good friends over time. And James fit in with all of them seamlessly, cracking jokes, laughing and soon teasing along with Bryce as though they'd known each other for years.

By the time James and Julie got back to the hotel, she was

giddy with excitement. Before she'd met James and now her bio siblings, the whole situation had left her feeling bleak and as though there was no hope. She was destined to be alone all her life. But after meeting and getting to know them, it was as though something deep inside had shifted and she could see a future for herself. One filled with possibilities—perhaps even happiness.

Chapter Twenty-One

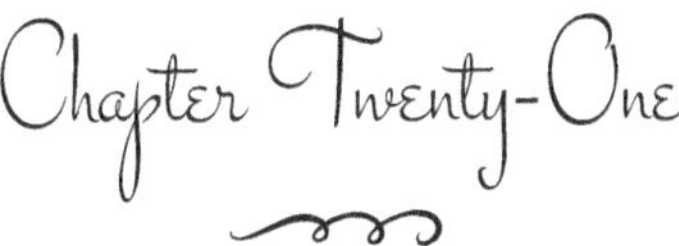

Matilda sat alone in a pile of rubble. The decision to knock down an unnecessary wall in the waiting room, opening the space up to how it had originally been constructed, had been hers. But now that she'd used a mallet to bring it down, she wasn't sure she'd done the right thing, and the job was only partially done. It was much harder work than she'd imagined it would be. What could be hard about smacking a wall with a mallet? Turns out, everything! *Everything* about it was extremely difficult, and she'd found herself breathless very quickly. She'd had to take a break every thirty seconds or so, leaning on the mallet to catch her breath.

Now that most of the wall was gone, apart from some stubborn framing, she sat in the middle of the rubble and surveyed the damage. This was all too much. Ryan had said she should hire someone to do this part, but she'd objected, saying she could do it and save them money. But now she realised he was right. She was out of her depth.

She couldn't do this. It was all too hard. What was she thinking, taking this on?

She stared at the mallet by her hand on the floor, willing

herself to pick it back up. But she was so tired. She pulled her phone from her pocket to call Ryan and tell him she was ready to hire some help, but it rang before she could.

Stella's cheery voice made her instantly feel better.

"Tilly! I miss you. What are you doing?"

She scrubbed her free hand over her face. "I'm tearing down a wall in the clinic and regretting my life choices. How about you?"

"Aw, you'll be okay. If anyone can do it, you can."

Stella had always been her loudest cheerleader. "Thanks, sis."

"How did your exam go? Are you officially an American vet now?"

"I passed, so I'm all registered. It's been a blur, honestly and I'm bone tired."

"Congratulations, that's fantastic. You always amaze me."

"You're very easily pleased," Matilda said with a yawn. "But thanks, I can't tell you good it is to talk to you right now."

"You'll never guess who I've just had dinner with," Stella said, in a smug voice. "Julie Brown!"

Matilda's breath caught in her chest. "What?"

"Yeah, I haven't had a chance to tell you but she called me a few days ago and asked if we could meet up."

"She's in Australia?"

"She came over with a friend for some kind of medical conference. James is really nice too. They're both lovely. We had such a nice time getting to know her. Even Todd liked her, which is a big deal, as you know." Stella laughed. She sounded happy.

Matilda bit down on her lip. It was hard to hear her sister talking about Julie this way. Julie didn't want anything to do with Matilda. She seemed to be holding the entire situation against her. But now she'd gone to Australia without saying anything about it. It hurt to be left out. Matilda's heart ached in her chest.

She was still playing catch-up. "I had no idea. I thought she was here. I saw her taking out the trash not long ago…"

"Listen to you! You sound American already."

"No I don't. I haven't been here that long. Why did she want to meet?"

"I guess to get to know us. You didn't tell me how alike we are! She looks so much like me, don't you think? We're definitely sisters. It was so exciting, finally getting to meet her. She even has a similar sense of humour and mannerisms. I can't believe those things can be genetic. It's incredible, really. We got along as if we'd all known each other forever."

As Stella gushed, Matilda grew more and more quiet. It wasn't fair. None of this was fair. She hadn't thought through the consequences of uncovering the truth this far. She'd realised it would impact her and had known that it could change her own relationship with her family members forever. But so far it hadn't seemed to do that, and she'd gained a whole new family as well. Stella had been cautious about it, but she'd brushed off her sister's concerns. Now she understood. Stella hadn't wanted to be replaced, and now Matilda felt the same way.

Chapter Twenty-Two

Rita stared at her cousin's red face. Sometimes she wondered how they'd ended up here, both working at the Honeysuckle Café alongside one another. Then she realised that she had no one to blame but herself. She'd done this. And right now, she regretted the choice.

"You always want everything your way! You just won't compromise, Rita! It's not fair. I'm supposed to be helping you, but how can I if you won't ever let me?"

"Cathy, we can't paint the dining room green. We don't have time to do that right now, and green doesn't exactly go with the theme. I prefer to keep things a bit more neutral. Then we can add splashes of colour with the décor."

"Green would be perfect in here. Don't worry about timing—I'll get them to paint overnight and take care of everything. You won't have to worry about it."

"It'll stink to high heaven! The customers won't want to eat the next day—they'll be overcome by fumes. We have to plan ahead if we're going to do any kind of renovations like that. We need to close down and get as many things done as possible so we're not interrupting business too often. We've done this once every few years for as long as I can remember."

"We'll use the low-scent paint, I promise. It'll be great." Cathy clapped her hands together, eyes sparkling. "And I think we should update the menus and some of these knickknacks to reflect the new colour scheme."

"All of that costs money, Cathy. Money we can't afford right now."

"It'll pay for itself, I promise you."

Rita sighed and threw her hands in the air. "Fine, you can do it. But if I hear customers complaining about the smell, or the overwhelming amount of green, I'm coming for you. Got it?"

Cathy grinned. "You won't regret it."

"I'm regretting it already," Rita mumbled as she shuffled through the café to her office.

As she sat in her chair, she let out an exhale of relief. Her eyes wilted shut, and she felt as though she could drift off to sleep in that position. But she wouldn't do that right now—she had things to do. Afterwards, she could go home and nap. It'd become something of a habit lately. The doctor had told her that she needed to take care of herself. Her immune system was compromised, and sleep helped to keep her strong.

"How on earth is this going to work?" she muttered to herself. She and Cathy couldn't be more different if they tried. Cathy was constantly getting on her nerves and making a nuisance of herself. And Rita was trying her best to get along, but she'd been the boss for so long now, it was hard to loosen the reins.

If it made Cathy happy, though, it was a small price to pay to be surrounded by green. Green, of all things! It was her least favourite colour. She huffed.

As Rita reached for the first bill on the pile, she noticed the stack of letters next to it. She'd been procrastinating a lot in recent years—she hated doing the orders and bill paying, the payroll and accounts. The ledgers were the bane of her existence. But this way, with the prospect of a letter to read when she was done for the day, it'd helped her get to it more efficiently, and she hadn't achieved so much in a long time.

With a frown of determination, she got to work. Before long, it was done, and she was able to open the next envelope. She smiled in anticipation. The last letter she'd read had left her with more questions than answers. She hoped this one written by her paternal grandmother would give her some kind of insight into her parents' life that provided more clarity.

To dear Raymond,

I'm not sure how you're making it through each day, but I wanted to write and encourage you. I'm sure Sylvia and the girls are well. She's with her parents in North Carolina and they love her and the girls, so I know they're well taken care of. But I heard the pain in your words when you wrote of how lonely it is for you, and how you long for them to come home. And I completely understand. I don't know if I could take it.

However, you must take it. This is your family, and you've got to do what it takes to fight for y'all to be together again. Bill made a mistake. I'm sure you can understand that. With so many long hours together working at the café, it was inevitable that he and Sylvia would be thrown together. And that he developed feelings for her was natural. However, the two of them having an affair right under your nose was a shock to me. A horrible shock. I feel so much anger on your behalf. I don't want to take sides, but I can't help it this time. They are in the wrong, and there is no getting around that.

What will you do?...

Rita put the letter down on her desk. Uncle Bill had an affair with Mom? Surely not. Mom loved Dad. They were married for fifty-plus years before they died. They were a good match. Dad was a grouch, of course. And Mom was a flake. But they made it work.

She rested her elbows on the desk and let her head fall into her hands. It all made sense now. The reason why Uncle Bill walked away from the café and left it all to her father. The reason they never spoke, even at the end of their lives. There was a family schism formed that was never healed. And it'd carried on to herself and Cathy even now, so many years later.

After a while, Rita packed up her things and drove back to the lake house. She got out of the truck and lumbered to the deck where her father's boat had been docked for all those years. The boat was still there, but it was out of the water, upside down and covered in a tarp. She could barely remember the last time she'd used it, and she wasn't physically capable of righting it now, or getting it back into the water. She felt so weak lately.

She sat on the bench beside the boat and stared out over the water, letting the memories wash over her like torrents of rain. Dad fixing the boat. Mom with a fishing pole extended over the edge of the water as she recounted some tale to Dad, like the day Rita got caught in a thunderstorm and Mom had to dry her off before she trekked mud through the kitchen, or that time Helen brought home a boy from school who looked like he'd recently joined a street gang, almost giving their parents a heart attack. Mom had greeted him with a colourless face, and Dad had immediately started cleaning his shotgun at the kitchen table.

Finally, the boy had stammered a goodbye and rushed out the door. They never saw him again, and Helen hadn't spoken to any of them for two days. Rita smiled fondly over the memories as they came, one by one, like pictures she'd looked through so many times before.

These letters had opened up the past in a way she hadn't expected and she wasn't sure how to process it all. There was no one to ask. No one who could answer her questions or clarify their contents. She had to put the pieces together herself and she was struggling to come to terms with the results. If only Helen were here. Helen would know what to do. She'd have said something light hearted to make Rita laugh and held Rita's hand as they talked it out. But Helen wasn't here and Rita had to face this all alone.

Chapter Twenty-Three

After a whirlwind week, the trip to Australia was over in a flash, and Julie was seated on the plane enjoying a business-class meal while watching yet another movie. She and James had spent the first few hours of the flight talking. Not about anything in particular, but everything and anything. Politics, religion, the weather, friendships, dreams, silly childhood stories. They never ran out of conversation, and it was the most relaxed friendship she'd had in years. Maybe ever.

The only thing that bothered her was the fact that he hadn't tried to kiss her. Not once. They'd held hands, very naturally, several times during the trip. He'd even placed his palm on the small of her back once when they were navigating a crowded sidewalk. But other than that, nothing. Maybe she was imagining the chemistry between them. Perhaps it was entirely one-sided. That made sense, actually, since he was a handsome, successful, kind and charming doctor while she was an unemployed hot mess with no idea what her future held, and long, straight hair that never seemed to quite fit any particular style.

Soon the plane landed, and they made their way through

customs. The entire way James made jokes that had her laughing, even though she was utterly exhausted and they almost couldn't find their luggage when directed to the wrong baggage carousel.

He made everything fun.

"I have a car coming to pick us up," he said as he tapped away on his phone.

"Oh, that's great. I thought we'd have to take an Uber or something, and I'm too tired to think clearly about where I'm going. I forgot Rita's address for a moment." Julie yawned so widely, she thought her mouth might crack open at the edges.

"No need for that. I've got you covered." He grinned at her. His blue eyes sparkled as they held hers. The way he looked at her, with so much affection, took her breath away. She couldn't look anywhere else but at him. She was certain he would take a step forward and cup her face with his hands. But he didn't.

Then he broke their connection with a cough. "I hope I'm not coming down with something. You feel okay?"

"I'm fine. But the plane definitely gave me a dry throat."

"We should hydrate when we get home."

"Good idea," she said, very aware of how hot her cheeks had become. They were probably bright pink.

As they climbed into the car, she relaxed against the leather seat with a sigh. "It's good to be home again."

"Did you enjoy the trip?" he asked.

She swivelled her head around to look at him. She hadn't slept much on the plane and was beginning to get to the stage where even a blink sent her into a semi-sleeping state. "I loved it. I had such a great time. It was a dream come true. I only wish we'd had more time."

"Me too," he replied. "I should've thought to book a vacation after the conference. But at least we had a couple of days together to enjoy ourselves when I was done."

"That hike through the rainforest to see the waterfalls was one of the highlights for me. That, plus the walk on the beach and dinner at that seafood restaurant. It was divine."

Their car pulled away from the curb.

"What about meeting your family?"

She nodded. "That was incredible. I guess I went into it not expecting much. I didn't know what they'd be like, or if they'd even want to meet me. I was prepared for the worst, I suppose. But they turned out to be so lovely and open to knowing me. And I had no idea how much like me they'd be. It really felt immediately like family."

"I liked them too," he said. "Hopefully you'll be able to stay in touch."

"I'm definitely going to do that. I want to go back and spend more time with them someday. And maybe they'll be able to visit here as well."

"What do you think Matilda will say about it?"

Julie's heart skipped a beat. She hadn't really thought much about it. In her mind, none of this had anything to do with Matilda. Of course, that was nonsense. "Do you think she'll be upset?"

"She might be. You didn't mention anything to her about it, did you?"

"No, I didn't."

"So, I guess be prepared that she could be upset about it. You didn't tell her you were going to meet her family. And you told me you've kind of been freezing her out, right?"

She nodded. "I have."

He offered her a sympathetic look. There was nothing more he needed to say. She could tell from his expression. Ignoring Matilda, shunning her and then rushing off to meet Matilda's siblings without telling her might have hurt her feelings. And she would be completely justified in being angry with Julie about it. The thought made her anxious. Before the trip, she didn't care what Matilda thought. She was the one who was hurt and angry. But now that she'd met the family in Australia, she realised how selfish she'd been.

For the rest of the drive, she sat in silence, pondering what she'd done and how she might talk to Matilda about it. Whether she should say anything to her, or just simply leave it alone. It would be much easier to pretend nothing had happened, although it was likely Stella had already told Matilda about her visit—the two of them seemed to be close.

When they pulled into the lake house driveway, it was pitch dark. There was a light on over the front porch, but the rest of the house was quiet and dimly lit. No doubt Rita was already in bed, since it was late. Julie couldn't wait to climb into her own bed in the guest room.

James walked her to the door with her luggage. They stood beneath the yellow porch light, looking at one another. Julie's hands were linked together in front of her cardigan. James' hands were on his hips. He took a step closer to her until there was barely any space between them. His gaze found hers, and the smile on his face faded. His eyes seemed to flash.

"Thanks for the trip. I can never repay you for it," Julie said quietly with a little bubble of laughter.

"No need to repay it. It was my pleasure. I had a really good time with you. You made the trip much more enjoyable than it would've been without you."

"Do you have work tomorrow?" she asked.

"One more day off. I'll probably sleep and do laundry."

"Enjoy..." Her voice faded away. She kept waiting for him to kiss her, or hold her, or at least close the small gap between them.

He took a step closer again until she could feel his body heat. He raised a hand to her cheek and cupped it for a single moment, then leaned down and kissed her other cheek.

Her lips tingled, waiting, waiting. But the kiss never came.

When he stepped back, his gaze flitted away. "Have a great sleep."

Then he walked back to the car. She watched it pull out of the driveway, her body still tingling from top to bottom. Then, with a shake of her head, she unlocked the door and stepped inside.

Chapter Twenty-Four

It was good to get away. The renovations on the clinic had been underway for a whole month, and Matilda was utterly exhausted. Tired to her core. She'd never been this tired in her life. And today, there were subcontractors on site, working on the electrical and the tiling. She'd only be in the way if she were there. Since it was a Saturday, September was almost over, and the weather was turning cooler, she and Ryan had decided to drive to northern Georgia and hike at Wildcat Creek in the Smoky Mountains.

It was early morning, and she yawned as they pulled away from the gas station where they'd purchased a red-hot (a flaky biscuit filled with a spicy sausage) and a cup of coffee each. The red-hots were delicious, although it seemed obvious they weren't healthy. But Ryan loved them, and he'd brought her around to his way of thinking. She wasn't sure anything purchased from a gas station could be good for a person to eat, but she was gradually becoming more Americanised with each passing day. And red-hots were something she had given up resisting.

With a sip of hot coffee, she took a bite of biscuit and let her eyes drift shut as she fought back the sleep that she so desperately needed.

"I'm so glad we're getting away today. I could sleep all day, but having a break is almost as good."

"You deserve it. I only wish I could whisk you away for a nice long vacation. But the timing..."

"The timing is terrible, the sentiment is wonderful. I'll look forward to that when the clinic is up and running smoothly."

He glanced over at her with an arched eyebrow. "And how long will that take?"

She groaned. "I have no idea. But we can imagine ourselves lying on the beach in Hawaii as a motivation to keep going."

"I like it," he replied with a grin.

It took just over two and a half hours to drive from Covington to Greer County in South Carolina. They stopped in Greenville for a bathroom break, then headed into the Smoky Mountains. They parked in a lot on one side of the road, then crossed over to the trail. It was a pretty trail, and it'd been a long time since Matilda had been hiking out in nature. The area was wooded with yellow poplar, red maple, aspen and pine. Pine needles, dead leaves, sticks and other foliage carpeted the forest floor.

The trail wound around the clear creek, up and over hills and around rocky outcroppings. They set out at a brisk pace. Matilda felt joyful as the cool, clean air filled her lungs and the sounds of traffic faded into nothing. Instead, all they could hear were the sounds of the forest and the quiet stillness of nature all about them. It was peaceful. And it was exactly what she needed.

As they walked, she started to think about her life and the swift direction change she'd made in the past year. There was a pang of homesickness and a little sadness over missing her family and home. She'd been living in the USA now for over a year, and she never expected to be gone for that long. Soon, she'd experience her second Thanksgiving and Christmas season. She loved it—the cold weather, colourful leaves and holiday spirit. It was her favourite time of year. But she had a lot of work to do before then.

"I've always wanted to do the Appalachian Trail," Ryan said suddenly.

"What's that?"

"It's close to here. And if you take the trail, you can walk for six months all the way up to Maine."

"To Maine?" she asked, eyes wide. "That's a long walk."

"I'd love to do the whole thing. It's always been a dream of mine."

"Maybe we can do it together one day."

He stopped walking and turned to look at her. "You'd walk for six months with a backpack carrying everything?"

She shrugged. "Sure. I've done backpacking before. Not for that long, of course. But it sounds like an adventure."

He laughed. "You're full of surprises."

Hours later, they were done and seated on Ryan's truck's tailgate at the car park. Matilda felt good. Revitalised. Her body was fatigued, but her mind was fresh. They drank some water and changed shoes, since both pairs of boots were coated in mud. Then they climbed into the truck to drive to one of Ryan's favourite restaurants that he'd promised to take her to for a late lunch.

The Dillard House was a stone restaurant set on the side of a mountain overlooking a valley. Curved windows displayed large timber tables surrounded by glowing golden lamplight. It was a magical place that immediately put Matilda at ease. Now that she'd cooled from her walk, she found herself shivering as she made her way into the restaurant. But inside, it was immediately warm with a fire glowing in the hearth on one wall.

It was midafternoon, and many of the tables were filled

with people finishing up their meals while they sipped after-lunch cocktails, wine or coffee. Conversations hummed, interspersed with gales of laughter. Some diners were dressed up. Others wore their hiking gear, much like Ryan and Matilda. The general atmosphere was one of fun and conviviality. The scents that filled the air were to die for.

"I'm starving," Matilda said, even as her stomach growled.

"Good, because there's going to be a lot of food." Ryan guided her to a table with his palm on her back.

When the waitress walked past them, Matilda raised a hand, but she didn't see her.

"What will you get?" Matilda asked as she lowered her hand and tapped her fingers on the tabletop. Her stomach was clenching with hunger, and she wasn't sure how long she could manage to wait for the food before she passed out.

"They have a set menu," he replied. "It's family style — they bring out the dishes and place them on the table. You serve yourself what you want."

"Oh, wow. That's awesome."

Soon they were able to order. She asked for sweet tea and some bread rolls to get them to started. At least it might tide her over until the main meal arrived.

When the bread rolls arrived at their table, she hungrily slathered one with honeyed butter and took a huge bite. Ryan laughed at her.

"I guess I should've packed snacks for you."

She swallowed her mouthful. "You know I have to eat frequently."

He laughed again. "I'll remember that. Speaking of eating, my parents want to have us over for a meal."

"I guess that's fair enough, considering we haven't seen much of them since the wedding." Although, she was nervous at the prospect. She'd met them briefly before and got the impression that they were a force to be reckoned with. They were high energy, confident and outspoken. She wasn't entirely sure that they liked her. She couldn't much blame them, considering she'd married their son for a green card. They couldn't know that the two of them were also in love, since they hadn't even admitted that to themselves at the time.

"They invited us to lunch on Saturday."

Her breath caught in her throat. That was awfully soon, but she had to face his family at some point, even if they did make her nervous. She wanted to get to know them. She hoped they'd grow to love her, but it might take some time.

The food arrived quickly. Southern-fried chicken, country ham, squash casserole, corn on the cob, coleslaw, calico salad, corn bread, and more. It filled up the round timber table and left Matilda's mouth watering.

"Let's eat," Ryan said, reaching for the chicken as Matilda excitedly began to fill her plate.

Matilda wondered what a Merritt family gathering would be like. She marvelled at how strange it was to be married to a man whose family she barely knew. She and Ryan had done things the wrong way around. She knew that now. But she never could've predicted they'd fall in love and want to stay married. If she could do it over, she'd have met the family first and had a real wedding. But there was no going back. And now she'd have to attend Ryan's family BBQ with a big smile on her face and hope they wouldn't hold it against her.

Chapter Twenty-Five

Rita had spent the past few weeks in a kind of daze. The information she'd uncovered in the old stack of letters had unsettled her spirit. She hadn't told anyone what she discovered and wasn't sure she wanted to. Her parents were gone now. She had no desire to sully their memories. But it had changed the way she saw them, and she couldn't undo that now.

She sat in the den at the lake house, in the semi-dark with only a single lamp to light the room. A photo album lay on the coffee table in front of her. She bent forward to retrieve it and flicked through the pages again. She'd already done this three times in the past hour, and every time she did, sadness washed over her. She saw everything with new eyes now.

A photo of the family at Six Flags. Another one at a family wedding. Still more when they went camping in north Georgia. Or that time they all went to Perry's in Daytona Beach for vacation for a week, and it felt like the most luxurious vacation she'd ever experienced. All of these images looked different to her now.

Her father had always been a grouch. She referred to him

as Oscar. It had been a fun joke, a *Sesame Street* reference. But perhaps there was a reason for his recalcitrance. Something she'd never understood before. He was in pain, and the knowledge of that sent a piercing stab through her heart. If only she'd known, she wouldn't have joked. She would've given him a hug, told him she loved him and that everything would be okay.

Because it was. In the end. The two of them stayed married. They didn't give up on one another. And they were happy. At least, that's what Rita had always thought. Maybe she was wrong about that too.

She pulled the album closer to look more deeply at the photographs from Six Flags Over Georgia—her favourite theme park. Roller coasters were so much fun back then. She couldn't imagine anything worse now. Riding one at her age would probably snap her neck like a twig. She grimaced as she considered it.

The first image was of herself and Helen, holding ice cream cones. They were about to drip, the weather was so hot that day. She vaguely remembered the sweat running down her back as she stood in line, sweltering as they waited their turn.

The next image had the whole family in it. Someone else must've taken the photograph, but she couldn't recall who it was. Likely someone passing by had offered. They stood in front of a roller coaster. Helen had an arm around Rita's waist. Rita's arm was casually slung around her sister's shoulders. They both pulled a face at the camera, but it was her father's face that drew her attention now. He stood with arms folded, his visage thunderous. Her mother was about as far away from him as she could manage while remaining in the frame. Her hands were threaded together, one knee bent, her chin down. She looked sorry. That's what it was. And Dad was furious.

All in a flash, the memory came rushing back. They'd eaten lunch at the cafeteria—burgers and fries with milkshakes. Mom dropped her chocolate milkshake on the ground. It hit the pavement and sent chocolate milk flying in every direction. It'd wet Dad's socks and shoes, and all up his shins. He'd exploded at her.

"Look what you did! You don't think about anyone but yourself!"

At the time, Rita had rolled her eyes. Typical Dad, overreacting. She'd taken her mother's side and given Dad the cold shoulder for the rest of the day. But maybe his words had meant more at that time than she'd realised. Her mother was unfaithful. She hadn't known that, but he would've been aware of it in this photo since they'd gone to Six Flags soon after they returned from North Carolina. She remembered it so clearly. It'd been Mom's idea—a way to reunite the family after a long separation by doing something fun together. Something they could remember. Mom was always saying things like that—"We're making memories."

Suddenly she realised there were tears on her cheeks. So many regrets. So much she wished she'd had a chance to say. She'd held resentment towards her father for years because of his temper. She thought he'd driven Mom away when they left Atlanta for those long months, but now she knew differently. Still, maybe he'd driven Mom away long before, and she'd found solace in his brother's arms. And maybe she'd paid for that decision the rest of her life.

Uncle Bill and Auntie Shelby had moved away after they got back from North Carolina. She hadn't realised there was a connection at the time. But they'd moved to Florida a couple of months later and the two families had hardly crossed paths again until after Uncle Bill's death. She wondered if Auntie Shelby ever knew the truth. It seemed Cathy didn't have a clue.

She wiped the tears from her cheeks just as Julie arrived home from her date with James. The two of them had been going out steadily for the past month, although Julie hadn't talked much about him, so Rita had no idea how it was going, and she didn't want to pry.

"What's wrong, Aunt Rita?" Julie asked, hurrying over to squat by the armchair.

Rita smiled through a veil of tears. "Oh, nothing, honey. Don't you worry about me. I'm just crying over memories." She tapped the photo album. "Doesn't your mama look sweet in this one?"

Julie sighed, and her worried expression turned to a sad smile. "She sure does. Where was that?"

"This was one of the many family weddings. I couldn't tell you whose. But I know she fought Mama tooth and nail over that dress. She hated to wear a dress at that age, and this one has a big white bow in back. She didn't want to wear that thing, and Mama was determined to make her. 'Course, Momma won in the end." Rita chuckled.

As Julie left to take a shower, Rita watched her go. How much life Julie had ahead of her—so many adventures to undertake, promises to make, lives to change. But not for Rita. She knew her best days were behind her. Almost all she had now were memories, and those memories were being challenged. It was too much to contemplate further, so she slapped the album shut and flicked off the light switch. Time for bed.

Chapter Twenty-Six

It was Sunday night. Julie had gone out with James the previous evening, but he'd called again that morning after church to see if she was free tonight. There was something he wanted to talk about. She'd begun to think that he really only wanted a friendship. He continued to ask her out, to pay for dates, to open the car door. But he still hadn't kissed her or even brought up a conversation about a future between the two of them. It was very confusing. Perhaps tonight he'd finally tell her what he was feeling.

She dressed in jeans and a sweater. It was a casual dinner, and the air had turned cooler lately. She loved jeans weather and was happy to have summer behind her. The past month had been a whirlwind. She'd begun helping out at the café, since Matilda was there less often. And between that, taking care of Rita, and spending time with James, she found herself busy for the first time in a while. It was a nice change, but it was also good to move on to a new stage or season of life.

The pain of her new family situation had faded a little, and she was almost ready to talk to Matilda. Almost, but not quite. She wasn't sure exactly why, but she felt as though talking to

Matilda face-to-face about everything would make it even more real and she might not be able to cope with the emotion of it. It didn't make sense, but it was how she felt.

When James picked her up, she was happy. She'd found someone whose company she loved and who seemed to feel the same way about her. She was excited to get up in the morning, thrilled when she got a chance to see him. The past had been blown apart by Matilda's revelations, but the future was looking brighter by the moment. She could almost start planning for it again.

"What did you get up to today?" she asked.

He smiled as he pulled the car out of the drive. "I went for a bike ride with some buddies."

"How far did you go?"

"About fifty miles," he replied.

She swallowed. "See, you *look* normal and then you say something like that."

He laughed. "It's normal for me. How about you?"

"Church with Rita. Then laundry and housework. I've started meal prepping on Sundays to get us through the week. Now that I'm at the café more and more, I need quick and easy things to make for meals."

"Sounds like a busy day. Maybe I can come to church with you next week?"

She grinned. "That would be nice."

They decided to eat at *Chili's*. Julie loved the bottomless chips and salsa, and she snacked on them while James told her about his ride.

"I wish I were that fit," she complained.

He shrugged. "It's not such a big deal on a road bike. It virtually propels itself."

"Sure. I totally believe you." She crossed her eyes at him, and he laughed.

When their burritos arrived, Julie cut hers into small

pieces before she began to eat, and he made fun of her. They had an easy relationship. They teased one another, were open about everything going on in their lives. The past couple of months had been such a balm to her soul, she could never fully express to him how much he'd done to save her from her own despair. She was about to try when he spoke up.

"I wanted to talk to you."

She nodded, encouraging him on.

"As you know, I've been at the same hospital for a number of years now. I love it there. They're really good to me, and I enjoy the work. It's so fulfilling. But at the same time, if I want to move my career forward, I have to be constantly on the lookout for opportunities. And I found one."

This conversation wasn't going the way she'd expected or hoped it would. She tried to reorient herself around what he was saying. What *was* he saying?

"Okay . . .?"

He inhaled a slow breath. "I applied for a job at a hospital in Boston. It's a big deal. A huge step up for me and an opportunity to do far more research than I'm currently doing. I interviewed for it a couple of weeks ago, and they called me on Friday to offer me the job."

"A job? In Boston?" He'd known about this last night and didn't say anything? She'd thought their date was so perfect. She'd flown home on wings. And now...

"Yes, I told them I'd think about it. But I'll probably accept. Unless you can think of a reason why I shouldn't..." He hesitated, watching her.

She was thrown off course. She'd thought he wanted to talk about their relationship. Where it was going. How he felt about her. What their future might look like together. And instead, he was here to discuss his career trajectory? That he was moving to Boston? What?

She stammered. "Uh, oh, okay. Well, it sounds like a good

opportunity." What else could she say? He'd interviewed for this job after they'd begun spending time together. And although she hadn't taken the step of calling him her boyfriend, considering they'd never had "the talk" and he hadn't kissed her yet, she'd been under the mistaken assumption that was the direction they were headed.

He ran fingers though his hair and leaned back in the booth. "Oh, okay. Well, thanks."

Was he upset? Had she said the wrong thing? This couldn't be happening. She'd been so happy, thinking something was finally going to work out in her life. That maybe she could look forward to the future again and let go of the past.

"I'll definitely miss you," she said.

And she swore a look of disappointment flashed over his face.

Chapter Twenty-Seven

The drive to Ryan's family home was a nerve-wracking one. Matilda looked out the window, letting her thoughts drift. Her fingers tapped out a rhythm on her knees. Behind the wheel, Ryan glanced over in her direction.

"Nervous?"

She nodded.

He sighed. "There's no need to be. My family isn't going to bite. Well, not hard, anyway."

She huffed. "Thanks. That's so helpful."

He laughed. "Sorry, I couldn't help it. But you'll be fine. It's going to be fun. Relax and enjoy yourself."

She wanted to. She really did. But it was intimidating, facing the whole brood at once. She'd asked if maybe they could start with his parents, but it was going to be the whole extended family. A BBQ to mark Labor Day, even though that had passed weeks earlier. His parents had been in Florida on vacation, and so this was the first weekend they'd had available to celebrate.

It took almost three hours to get to his parents' place in eastern Georgia. They lived on a property near Statesboro. It was where Ryan had grown up—a farm specialising in timber and horses. He'd raised horses since he was young, and Matilda was actually excited to see some foals. She hoped they'd have a few around. She loved horses but had never had much to do with them.

The driveway was long and straight. It passed through an avenue of pine trees. Beyond that were acres and acres of pines —tall, straight and green, planted in rows. Closer to the house, there were fields where horses grazed. And it wasn't long before Matilda spotted a few foals on gangly legs, lolloping around the place playfully.

"Look! They're so sweet!" she cried, pointing them out.

Ryan nodded. "You'll get to meet them. I'll take you out later."

They pulled up beside a long, low white house. There was an old tractor parked nearby under a big oak tree, and several pallets stacked next to it. Beyond that was a massive old barn painted red, with tall round hay bales piled alongside it.

Three dogs raced out to greet them, barking furiously as Ryan parked the truck. He climbed out, and their barks turned to keening as he greeted them one by one. Then some figures emerged from the house and meandered towards them.

A large man with bowed legs shook Ryan's hand. Then a rotund woman with an apron tied about her waist and wearing a polka dot dress threw her arms around him with a great smile on her lips.

"Mom, Pop, you remember Matilda?"

They both nodded and came to greet her with a tentative handshake. She smiled and moved closer to Ryan. "Thanks for inviting us. Your farm is beautiful."

"Thank you so much," Lynette, his mother, said. "You're too kind."

Bob, his dad, beamed at her. "Glad you could make it. Was the drive okay?"

"It was fine," Ryan said, putting his arm around Matilda protectively. "Matilda made a cake."

"Oh, how thoughtful," Lynette said.

Matilda pulled the cake from the back seat of the truck and handed it to Lynette. "It's an English teacake. My mother's recipe."

"Well, bless your heart. Come on inside, you two. Everyone's excited to see you."

There was a gang of kids chasing one another around the outside of the house. A couple of them cried greetings to Ryan without slowing their pace. He laughed at them and lunged in the direction of one of the boys, who jumped out of his way with a squeal.

Inside, the house was loud—so many voices, all raised in conversation. Country music played on a stereo in the corner of the living room. There was a long trestle table in the centre of the room, piled with food and drinks. People held small paper plates or red plastic cups.

Bob turned down the music and raised a hand before yelling "Hey!" Everyone stopped talking midsentence and turned towards him. "Let's welcome Ryan and his new bride, Matilda. Come hug their necks when you can." Everyone broke into applause. A few whistles resounded. Then he turned the music back up in volume, and the conversations resumed.

Matilda's heart thudded inside her chest. There were a lot of guests, more than she'd thought. Surely this couldn't all be family. "Who are these people?" she whispered to Ryan.

He laughed. "Some are neighbours, and the rest are family."

"There's no way I can remember all these names."

"No need. I'll run interference for you."

"Don't leave me," she demanded, sliding her arm through his.

"I've never seen you this shy," he said.

She shrugged. "I feel really guilty about marrying their golden-haired child without telling them. And I'm sure they all hate me."

"Now you're being paranoid. No one hates you. I promise you that. And anyone who gives you trouble will have to deal with me."

His words helped her feel a little better. She let the tension ease from her shoulders and did her best to relax. They got cups of sweet tea from the drinks station, and she loaded a small plate with chips and dip, pigs in a blanket, and some kind of meatball with BBQ sauce. Then they wandered around, chatting with people.

Everyone was very friendly, and she started to realise she'd built up the issue in her own mind. It seemed no one was upset with her, or wanted to tear her apart after all. She'd clearly imagined a scenario far worse than reality.

A few hours later, most of the guests had left. The noise died down in the house, and Matilda got to work helping her mother-in-law clear dishes from the trestle table.

"Ryan tells me you're a vet," Lynette said as she cleared a plate of potato salad.

"That's right. I've purchased a vet clinic, and I'm renovating it."

"That sounds like a lot of work."

"It is. I've got sore muscles in places I didn't know existed." Matilda groaned.

Lynette chuckled. "Hard work does the soul good."

"I'm sure you and Bob would know about that, having worked a farm so long. Do you still enjoy it?"

Lynette shrugged. "We wouldn't know what else to do with ourselves. It's our life."

They set the dishes in the kitchen. Matilda glanced around

at the mess in dismay. "Wow. Let me help you with these dishes."

"That would be wonderful. Thanks, hon."

They got started on washing up while Ryan and a few others helped clear the rest of the table and put away the leftover food. Lynette rinsed while Matilda stacked the dishwasher. The kitchen was huge, with an enormous gas stove in the centre of the room that also housed a furnace to heat the home. Large windows looked out over the horse paddock and the big oak tree.

"You know, we never thought Ryan would get married the way he did."

Matilda's heart constricted. She inhaled a sharp breath as she tried to formulate a response in her mind. "I know you didn't…"

Lynette turned to face her, pain in her eyes. "We can't fathom it."

"I'm sorry…"

"He says your parents are deceased?"

"That's right."

"So, I can understand you not having family there. Maybe the pain is still raw for you. But we're here, nearby. We could've come. A phone call…" Her voice broke, and tears filled her eyes.

A lump formed in Matilda's throat. "I know…"

"He's our only son, you know. We wanted to be at his wedding. I've dreamed of it for years. I wanted him to find love, to be happy, to have a family. And now…"

Matilda felt helpless. She didn't know how to respond. Lynette had a point. She knew it. It's why she'd dreaded coming to see them. She was in the wrong. She'd married Ryan impulsively and because she wanted a visa. He'd been the one to suggest the arrangement but she could've turned him down. Lynette and Bob had missed out on their only son's wedding because of her.

She put a hand on Lynette's arm. "I'm truly sorry, Lynette. I know it must've hurt to find out what we did. I promise it was simply a spontaneous decision, and we didn't think through the implications. But I do regret it—I wish we'd waited and done things in a more thoughtful way. I didn't really get to enjoy my wedding either because it happened so fast. I wish I could do it all again."

Lynette sniffled. "Maybe you could."

"What?"

"You could renew your vows. Have the family there. Wear a dress and cut the cake, the whole nine yards."

Matilda frowned. "Have the wedding again?"

Lynette began to smile. "Yes, do it right this time."

Matilda hesitated. "I suppose we could do that." Would that work? Would it help everyone to feel better about the situation? Because she desperately wanted to make up for any hurt they'd caused.

"There's no reason you couldn't."

"That's true, I guess." Matilda offered a faltering smile. "It might be fun."

Lynette beamed. "Wonderful! We're having a wedding. Oh, I'm so excited." She patted Matilda's hand. "It's going to be great. Wait until I tell Bob. He'll flip."

Chapter Twenty-Eight

Two weeks later, it was mid-October, and Rita was partway through another round of chemotherapy. This time she was losing hair, and she wasn't happy about it. She'd taken to wearing a bandana tied around her head. She felt like a hippie. It wasn't the kind of look she'd usually go for, but she was doing her best to stay positive and embrace it.

In the past month, Cathy had followed through on her promise to repaint the dining area in the café. It was green, and it looked surprisingly good. Rita paused to look the place over. There weren't many customers yet—the rush hadn't started. There were new potted plants that matched the new green paint, several of the photographs Rita had found from the cafe's early days hung on the walls, as well as some modern pieces of art that were surprisingly good, even if Rita wouldn't have picked them herself. She had to admit that the décor had been updated in a way that was fashionable and fresh. Something she hadn't expected from her cousin, given the way Cathy generally dressed—as though she was a disco roller-skating champion who'd teleported into the future directly from the year 1980.

"What do you think?" Cathy asked from behind her.

Rita spun to face her. "I like it."

Cathy looked unconvinced. "Really? I know it's not your style..."

"I wouldn't have picked it myself, but you've done well. It's come together nicely and I do think it improves the space—you were right."

Cathy's lips pulled into a smile. "Thanks, Rita. I appreciate that."

"You've got a gift, Cathy. You should consider exploring that."

"I will." She was beaming now. "I'm working on the menu and..."

Rita frowned. "Hold on right there. I'm not ready for any more changes yet. Can you please let me absorb the most recent ones before you start looking for more to do?"

Cathy sniffed. "I suppose so. I swear, Rita, you're sounding more and more like our grandmother with every passing day."

"A high compliment," Rita said, raising her chin. "Now, I'm heading home for a rest. You're in charge—which I know is music to your ears."

"I think that's a great idea. You're looking a little pale."

"Truth be told, I'm not at my best today. But I'm glad you're here to manage things for me."

Cathy nodded. "You don't have to worry about a thing."

"But I will anyway."

Then Rita gave Cathy an uncharacteristic hug, startling her cousin into silence. She shuffled out of the café with a grin on her face.

What would Cathy think if she knew what Rita had discovered about their parents? She hated to imagine. As she drove, she went over the details in her mind again and again.

How did it happen? Was Mom feeling neglected? Did Uncle Bill have marriage problems? Were they simply thrown together and an attraction grew? Why would they both be willing to risk losing their families for the sake of a brief affair? And how had they managed to put it behind them and stay married to their spouses for the rest of their lives?

She pulled into the driveway at the lake house and climbed slowly out of the car. Her head was light, and it took a mammoth effort to walk into the house. She set her purse down on the hall table and then held on to it as a dizzy spell passed. With her eyes shut, she willed herself to get moving. If only she could make it to the bed and lie down. She'd be better after a nap.

"Aunt Rita, are you okay?" Julie's voice was laced with worry.

"I'm a little dizzy, but I'll be okay in a moment. I need to lie down."

Julie's hands lifted Rita's arm until she was cupping her elbow with one hand, an arm around her waist to support her. "I'll help you to bed."

"Thank you, honey. You're such a blessing."

As they walked together down the hallway, Julie spoke again. "I think you should call the doctor. Get a check-up."

"I'm sure that's not necessary."

"It'd help me feel better about things."

Rita chuckled. "Well, if it helps you feel better, then I guess I should do it."

"Thank you. I'll call him for you tomorrow, if you like."

"That'd be fine."

"And just as soon as you lie down, I'll start on some chicken soup for dinner. Would you like that?"

"That would be perfect, honey."

Julie helped her into bed, took off her shoes, and pulled

the covers up for her. Then she kissed Rita's forehead and tiptoed from the room. Rita wanted to cry over how sweet her niece was, and how well she was looking after her, but she was far too tired to expend energy on tears. And within minutes, she was fast asleep.

Chapter Twenty-Nine

The next day, Julie called the hospital and was instructed to bring Rita in. So, she drove Rita to the hospital fully intending to keep out of the way so that she wouldn't have to see James. He'd told her he was taking the job in Boston, and she'd been dodging his phone calls and not replying to his texts since. His last text sounded a little sad, but she wasn't ready to speak with him yet.

> Are you busy? I haven't heard from you in a
> few days.

That was it, two days ago. Nothing since. She was being childish. She recognised that. But his words had hurt her deeply, and she didn't know how to address him yet. She needed time to think it through. What should she say? How should she react? Clearly, he had a very different idea about their ongoing relationship than she did. It seemed he thought of her as some kind of friend that he took on platonic dates while she'd been humming "*Here Comes the Bride*" in her head with a goofy grin plastered across her face on the daily.

She was wrong. She'd let her feelings get away from her,

something she didn't generally do. Usually she was reserved, careful with her heart. But she'd trusted him, and he'd hurt her. She hadn't said anything to Rita about it yet. Her aunt had enough going on in her life—she didn't need to worry about Julie any more than she already did.

One thing that all of this had done, though, was give her back her resolve. She would return to college in the new year to complete her qualifications. She'd needed a break, and she'd had one. An entire semester off should be enough. After the holidays, she'd be ready to return. She already felt more motivated after her vacation in Australia—meeting her family had helped heal some of the wounds.

At the hospital, she got Rita situated in the oncology department and then went on the search for a cup of hot chocolate or something else she could drink. She was parched and looking for an excuse to get away from the place where she was most likely to run into James. As luck would have it, he found her at the vending machine anyway.

"Julie," he said as he jogged towards her along the wide hallway.

She squeezed her eyes shut and inhaled a quick breath. His voice made her heart race and her stomach drop. Then she spun to face him with a vacant smile.

"James. There you are. I wondered if you were nearby. I had to bring Rita in for a checkup."

"I'm headed over there now to see her. Running a bit late. Can I talk to you for a minute? It'll be quick, since I'm..."

"Running late. I heard," she said. "Sure, we can talk. What's up?" She attempted a casual, light tone. The last thing she wanted was for him to know that he'd hurt her.

Her heart was in her throat. His blue eyes sparkled as though he was happy to see her. Why did things have to be so difficult?

He leaned one hand against the vending machine. He was

so close to her, she could smell his aftershave. It made her giddy,.

"I've been trying to call you."

"I'm sorry. It's been crazy lately."

"That's what I figured. And my texts…"

"I'm terrible at texting. Sorry again."

He arched an eyebrow. "Really? You weren't so bad at it a few weeks ago."

She sighed. "James…"

"What? We can be straight with one another, surely. Tell me what's wrong."

Her throat tightened. She didn't want to cry. It would be humiliating, and he'd think she was crazy. But how could that make things worse? He was leaving. She might never see him again. And he hadn't even given her a second thought.

"I guess I'm confused. I thought we were…"

"What?"

"More than friends. I thought we were getting to know one another again, and maybe you had feelings for me in the same way that I have for you. But obviously I was wrong about that, so I'm just taking some time to process it. I'm sorry I haven't texted you back."

His eyes narrowed. "Now I'm confused."

"You're leaving," she said. "You're taking a job in Boston and leaving. I might never see you again. And you didn't consider me in that decision. I thought we were on a trajectory… but I was wrong. I was so wrong. I don't know why I thought that—you haven't even tried to kiss me. That should've been the only thing I needed…" She was cut off by the look on James' face.

His jaw clenched, and he stepped closer to her. "You weren't wrong…"

She backed away from him, chin jutting out. "Leave me alone, James. You really hurt me."

She spun away, already striding for the oncology department without her hot chocolate.

He hurried after her, grabbed her by the arm, and pushed her into a small room, shutting the door behind them. It was dark in the room. There were bunk beds against one wall and a small desk at one end. A night-light glowed near the floor.

She backed up against the end of the bed—there was nowhere else to go. He crowded against her. She wished she could see his eyes, but it was too dark. She felt his presence, the tension between then sparking with electricity. Her heart thundered against her rib cage, and her breathing was rapid and shallow. She longed for him, her body aching for his touch.

"I didn't mean to hurt you," he whispered.

Then he pressed his lips urgently to hers, stealing her breath away. She was taken by surprise, but within a moment she responded, kissing him back. His arms encircled her firmly, and she found herself being pushed first against the bed, then the wall, as his kisses became more urgent. He pressed both hands to the wall on either side of her, then slowed his pace.

"I can't stand it when you treat me that way. You were cold out there. Like ice," he whispered against her lips.

She tried to catch her breath. What could she say? He'd finally kissed her, something she'd been dreaming of and hoping for, but he was leaving. Now it would only hurt more.

"What are you thinking?"

"That you're leading me on. You're moving to Boston. And I'm staying here—I have to. Keep away from me, James. I've had my heart torn into pieces already this year. I don't need you to make it worse."

She ducked out from beneath his arms, opened the door, and with one last glance back at his stricken face, she strode away.

Chapter Thirty

Back in the waiting room with Rita, Julie couldn't sit still. She'd perch on a chair beside Rita for a minute, then get back up again and stride across the room. Rita watched her in amusement.

"What's gotten into you?"

"Too much caffeine," Julie said, which was partially true. She'd drunk three cups of coffee that morning, an unusual amount even for her.

Finally, it was Rita's turn to have her name called, and the two of them were taken to a small room where Rita would be checked by the doctor. It would probably be James, since he already said he was on his way to see Rita. No doubt, Rita had waited this long because Julie had held up her doctor, although she had no intention of telling Rita that information.

The truth was, she couldn't get James' words out of her mind. Had she misunderstood everything? And that kiss... Where had it come from? Was it because she mentioned the lack of a kiss? She couldn't say. She was in tumult. And she had no idea what to think, feel or do.

The door opened, and James stepped through it. His cheeks were flushed, his hair mussed.

"Good morning, Rita. How are you feeling today?"

He checked her over and she mentioned her light headedness, that she wasn't feeling well. The hair loss was something Julie hadn't seen up close before since Rita always wore a scarf, and it was like a punch to her gut to see it. She hated to witness her aunt going through all of this pain and suffering. If she could do anything about it, she would. But she felt powerless.

After they were done, James lowered himself onto the edge of the bed where Rita sat, legs hanging, and spoke in a kind voice. "The treatment is going well. It's going to have some side effects, and I can help you with medication and suggestions to mitigate those. But you're doing really well. I'm happy with how we're progressing. We're seeing some good results. And I would encourage you to rest, take care of yourself, and keep doing what you're doing."

Rita sighed. "Thanks, James. That helps me feel a lot more confident."

"Let's stick with the plan. You have one last treatment tomorrow. We're getting close to our goal."

"Agreed," Rita said with a smile. "I can get through one more."

Julie told Rita she would meet her in the waiting room, then got up and walked out with a nod goodbye to James. She couldn't be in there any longer. So many emotions swirled around inside. Being so close to James after that kiss was hard enough. But watching Rita endure this awful disease was more than she could take right now. She strode down the hallway, arms crossed, in search of a place to sit quietly. She needed some time alone to think.

Chapter Thirty-One

It was the weekend, and Matilda wanted to spend the entire day in bed. But she couldn't. She and Ryan had to finish the renovations on the house. Ryan said it would give her a break from the clinic and he'd been working on it so long he wanted to finally get it done. It looked good. There was only a little landscaping left to go.

The fresh white paint gleamed. The new windows sparkled in the autumn sunshine. The house looked new on the outside and was stunning on the inside. She could say that because it had almost entirely been done by Ryan. She'd contributed very little, really. And he'd done a fantastic job. It was a dream house—three stories, open spaces, high ceilings, five bedrooms and three bathrooms, plus a large office for them both to share. She especially loved the gourmet kitchen with the large sliding glass doors that led out onto a porch that looked over the lake.

But another day of landscaping made her want to cry and hide under the covers. Every single part of her body hurt from the work she'd done all week on the clinic, and now she had to go outside in a pair of overalls and boots to help dig soil, plant saplings and lay sod. Ryan wanted the sod to take root before the cold weather arrived, but all she could think about was how little energy she had left to do anything at all.

She stumbled into the kitchen, aiming directly for the espresso machine. Ryan laughed. "You look tired. You should stay in bed today."

"No, I can't. You're landscaping."

"I know, but you don't have to help me if you don't want to."

"I want to. I can't leave you to do it all by yourself. That wouldn't be fair. You've done so much already."

"I don't mind." He looped his arms around her waist, pinning her to him.

She laughed. "I can't reach the coffee. I need the coffee."

He released her with a kiss. "If you're going to help today, you shouldn't push yourself."

"We're in this together." She poured coffee into a mug even as she yawned widely.

He laughed again. "This is going to go great. I can just tell."

When he yawned, she pointed at him. "See, you're tired too."

"We've had a really busy week at work."

"Maybe we should leave the landscaping until next weekend."

He shook his head. "Definitely can't do that. The sod has already been delivered, and it'll die."

"We should've hired someone."

"I got them to level everything. All we have to do is lay it out and water it. It'll be a piece of cake." He winked.

She sniffed. "Sure it will. I've heard you say that before— when I was about to demo the waiting room at the clinic."

"Oh, yeah. Sorry about that."

She gulped a mouthful of coffee. It burned on the way

down. She would have to drink more slowly. "Never mind—you can make it up to me later. Maybe we can go on an actual date next weekend, since all of the renovations will be done here and at the clinic. By the way, after that, I don't want to even hear the word 'renovation' again for as long as I live."

He grinned. "Not a big fan of it, huh?"

"It's safe to say that I will never again in my life renovate anything."

They spent the entire morning laying sod. Matilda's arms felt as though they might detach from her body, they were so sore and heavy. But she was determined not to complain, so she worked through the discomfort without a word.

She carried one of the last pieces of sod to an empty patch of dirt, but on the way, her foot caught on a stone and she stumbled forward, then fell onto the piece of sod. Her face pressed into the grass, and she breathed in the loose dirt. Her knee landed on a stone, and pain shot through it. She yelped in pain.

Ryan was hauling another piece of sod from the pile and turned to look at her. He laughed. "I'm going to name you Clumsy the Dwarf."

Rage burned inside her. She rolled onto her back and stared into the sky as her entire face became a blaze. Her stomach clenched, and she wanted to scream. How dare he say that to her when she was working so hard and hurt herself in the process?

She jumped to her feet and glared at him. "You're a jerk. You know that?" Then she stormed into the house, kicking her boots off at the door so she didn't track mud.

In the shower, her rage subsided, but she was still hurt by his words. He hadn't come to comfort her or checked to see that she was okay. Instead, he'd thought the whole thing was a big joke. But she was far too tired and sore to see the funny side of it.

She dried off, dressed, and went to the kitchen to fix herself a snack and an enormous glass of white wine. As she sipped the wine on the back porch, she breathed deeply and began to feel a little better and somewhat ashamed of her outburst. She was usually so controlled and didn't let her tongue get away from her like that. But she was on edge lately —tired, anxious and uncertain of whether everything she was doing was a gigantic mistake. She'd taken it out on him.

She heard Ryan come in and head to the shower but didn't turn around. Then after a while, he joined her on the deck, a beer in hand. He sat beside her with a grunt.

"Are you okay?" he asked.

Her eyes narrowed. "*Now* you ask?"

He smiled. "I didn't realise you'd hurt yourself. I'm sorry."

She stood up and walked over to him, then crawled onto his lap. His arms closed around her, and she snuggled against his chest. He was warm, and it felt good.

"I'm sorry too."

He kissed the top of her head. "Are we okay?"

"We're fine."

His steadfastness in the face of her harsh words was calming. He wasn't angry or offended. He was nothing like her ex, who wouldn't have spoken to her for days if she'd said something like that to him. Ryan was unflappable, solid, reliable. She could count on him to be there, even when she was struggling. He was everything she'd ever wanted and he was right there, wrapped around her. She could fall asleep in his arms, and he'd take care of her. She knew then that she'd made at least one right choice in her life so far.

Chapter Thirty-Two

Rita took a sip of tea and studied the edge of the lake where the water slowly lapped rhythmically against the bank. It was hypnotic. She'd always loved to watch the water—the ducks waddling around the edges or jumping in to swim with a wag of feathered tail. The water bugs dancing across the surface, the plop of a bass coming up to grasp one.

Her final treatment was done. She was spent, but it felt good to be at the end of it. Now they would wait to do the tests to see how it'd gone. Until then, she could relax. Rest, as her doctor suggested.

She picked up the phone to call Cathy at the café. She couldn't go in today—she didn't have the energy. But she wanted to check on them and make sure they were all okay. Julie was here with her. She hadn't been scheduled onto a shift. She'd driven Rita, and was currently working on putting together some cheese and crackers, not that Rita would be able to keep them down.

The phone rang, and it took Cathy a while to answer. Finally, she did.

"Hello?"

"Hey, Cathy. How's it going?"

Cathy's voice was bright. "You'll never guess who came in today."

"Who?"

"Tim... oh, darn... What's his name? You know that guy, that Tim guy?"

Rita frowned. "I can't think of any Tim. Not off the top of my head."

"Oh, this is frustrating. It's on the tip of my tongue. He's real famous. You know him. I'm sure you do."

"Oh, well, I'm glad you had a famous Tim come into the café. I hope you got a photo."

"Definitely—I had Amanda take one with me and Tim so we can hang it on the wall."

"We're not really a celebrity-on-the-wall kind of place..."

"You'll love it."

With a sigh, Rita chose not to pick that particular fight today. She didn't have the energy. If Cathy wanted to hang some random guy named Tim on the wall, she could have at it.

"So, everything's fine, then?"

"It's kinda slow, but everything's great. No issues here. How about you? Feeling okay?"

"I'm done with my treatments, so that's something. But I'm not feeling very well. I won't be in for a while."

"Don't you worry about us. We have everything under control here."

As she hung up the phone, Rita couldn't help being thankful for Cathy, something she'd never thought she would possibly think. But her cousin had really come through for her when she needed it, and she wouldn't forget that.

Julie slid the glass doors open and set a tray of cheese, crackers and glasses of sweet tea down on the small round table next to Rita.

"I know you're probably not hungry, but I brought this

out here for me, and if you'd like to try to eat, you're welcome to it."

"Thanks, hon. You're the best." Rita smiled up at her and took one of the glasses of tea to sip.

Julie piled cheese onto a cracker. She didn't say anything more. Rita knew her well enough to realise there was something on her mind. The furrow in her brow, the wistful stare into the distance—something was wrong.

"What's up, buttercup?"

Julie sighed. "I don't want to burden you."

"You're not a burden. I want to help. I need something to take my mind off my nausea. So, what's going on?"

"James kissed me."

"Well, hallelujah! It's about time." Rita chuckled softly. "What's the problem? Was it a bad kiss?"

"No, it was a great kiss. A truly great kiss." Julie hesitated. Rita waited. "The problem is that he's moving. He got a job in Boston."

"Really? Well, that's terrible timing."

"You're telling me! I can't go to Boston. And it's like he didn't even consider me in the equation. He just informed me that he was moving, like I was a friend who didn't figure into his thinking at all. But then he kissed me. So, now I'm totally confused. I have no idea what to do next."

"Have you spoken to him about this?"

"No, I can't talk to him. I don't know what to say. I don't even know how I feel."

Rita sipped her tea quietly for a few minutes. Finally, she said, "I think you do know how you feel, hon."

"Yeah, I guess you're right. I care about him. There—I said it. I like him. I want to be more than friends. He's just so great, in every way. And I thought we were on the same page. But he never made a move, and then said he was leaving. It wasn't until I pointed out that he hadn't kissed me that he finally did.

And so I can't be sure if it was in reaction to my words, or if he really wanted to… This whole situation is such a mess."

"Do you want some advice?"

"Yes, please. I'm dying for advice. I'm completely at a loss. I have my studies at UGA. I have you to take care of. I can't just leave here. But at the same time, I don't want to lose James. And even as I'm saying all of this, I still don't know what he wants." Julie looked at her, her lower lip trembling.

Rita cupped Julie's cheek with her hand a moment, then sat back in her chair to look at the sky. "We don't get a lot of chances to find love. I loved your uncle, you know. But I never found someone else who made me feel the same way after he died. And that's fine—I've made a good life for myself. But every now and then, I find myself wishing I'd made more of an effort. There was a man once who was interested in me. I liked him—more than liked him, really. But he lived in a different state, and I didn't want to give up the café to go over there. He couldn't give up his firm to come here. So, it never resulted in anythin'."

"Do you regret that?" Julie asked.

Rita nodded. "When you come to the end of things, or when it looks like you might be, you start ponderin' your life and the choices you've made. And one of my very few regrets was that moment—I should've said yes. I don't know if it would've worked out, but I should've at least tried. Given him a chance. Given *us* a chance because as much as I love the café, it's not the thing I've thought about lately—it's the relationships, the family members I don't see as often as I'd like, the romance I let slip away. Those are the things that matter. So, my advice is this—if he wants to move to Boston, and he wants you to go with him, you should do it. Life is short. You can study anywhere, hon. And I don't want to see you let go of something that could be great just because of me. I couldn't live with that."

Tears pooled in Julie's eyes. She dabbed at them with a napkin. "Are you sure?"

"I'm absolutely sure, honey. I'll be perfectly fine. I've so appreciated you being here for me during this time, but I don't want to hold you back. You have a whole life to live."

A big tear wound down one of Julie's cheeks, followed by another. "Thanks, Aunt Rita. I'll think about it."

"And talk to him. You've got to *communicate*."

"You're right. I will."

Chapter Thirty-Three

The next day, Julie decided to go fishing. It was something she'd done as a child whenever she needed to get away from the stresses in her life, and she hadn't done it in years. So, she rose early, went to the bait shop, and bought live bait. Then she sat down near the water's edge in a wicker chair and tossed her line into the lake. She probably wouldn't catch anything, but it was the action that mattered. Or the lack of it, in this case. She would simply sit, stare and think. It was the perfect activity for a Sunday afternoon while Rita napped inside the house.

The sun was warm on her skin, the air clean and the lake perfectly still. After a while, she heard a door shut and then footsteps nearby. She turned to see Matilda walking in her direction. She straightened in her chair, heart pounding. She'd meant to go and see Matilda at some point, but still hadn't gotten around to it. If she was honest, she was avoiding it. Avoiding her.

Matilda stood beside her, looked at the lake. "Catch anything?"

Julie forced a smile and stood up. "No, nothing yet."

"Can we talk?"

"Sure. I'll grab you a chair."

She handed Matilda the fishing pole to hold while she jogged up to the back deck to fetch another chair. Then she set it next to her own, and the two of them lowered themselves to sit side by side.

"What's up?" Julie finally asked.

"I know you went to Australia and met my siblings."

Julie nodded slowly. "That's right."

"You didn't say anything."

"I'm sorry. I should've told you."

"But you were angry..." Matilda replied.

Julie looked at her. "I was angry with you, but I know it's not your fault. So, I'm sorry for that."

"You're not angry now?"

"Nope. Not angry now."

Matilda issued a deep sigh. "I'm glad."

"Stella and your brothers are really nice. I liked them a lot."

"They're your brothers too now, I guess."

Julie blinked. "Yeah, you're right. I'm still trying to wrap my head around that. I always wanted siblings. Now I have them."

"I know you and I aren't actually siblings, but it kind of feels like it."

"I suppose that's true."

"I mean... we could pretend we are. Everyone else around here is related." Matilda snorted.

"That's true."

"You know, Stella went through a phase when we were young where she collected grasshoppers. It was a really scary time in my life. I never knew when an insect was going to leap onto me."

Julie laughed. "That sounds horrifying."

"It was. I'm still traumatised. I hate grasshoppers."

"What else can you tell me about them?"

They sat together for an hour talking. Matilda told Julie all about her childhood—what her parents were like, how it was to be raised with three siblings. And then Julie spoke about her mother, how her mother had coped after her father died, how they'd always been each other's everything. They both laughed, cried a few tears, and Julie found herself with a lump in her throat by the time Matilda waved goodbye to traipse back across the newly laid sod to her own house.

"It looks great, by the way!" Julie called after her.

Matilda nodded as she shut the gate behind her. "Thanks."

As soon as the door closed, Julie decided to pack up. The sun had dipped towards the horizon, it was starting to get cold, and not a single bite so far.

A car pulled into the driveway, its tyres crackling on the gravel. She glanced up to see James' car. He climbed out and looked around, his gaze finally resting on her. Then he walked in her direction. She set the fishing pole in the boathouse and was putting the tackle box away when he reached her.

"Hi," she said.

He nodded. "How are you?"

"Fine. You?"

"I'm okay, but I've been trying to reach you all afternoon. You haven't picked up the phone."

She dipped her head in the direction of the lake. "I was fishing."

"I see that. Can we sit?"

She nodded. They each sat. He pulled his chair close so that his knees were almost touching hers. She inhaled a quick breath. "So, what is it? What do you need to talk about so urgently?"

He frowned. "I think you know."

"The kiss?"

"The kiss, us, the fight we had. All of it. We need to talk about these things. You can't just ignore it and hope it goes away. Hope *I'll* go away."

"I don't want you to go away."

He reached for her hands and held them. "I'm glad to hear you say that. I know I need to explain. After what you said, I realised that I'd given you mixed signals. I never meant to do that. I wanted to take things slowly because I care about you. You were family to me for a really important part of my life, and I didn't want to mess that up by jumping into something too fast. Does that make sense?"

"I get it," she said. "But I wish you'd told me. I was so confused—I thought we were on the same wavelength, but then I wondered if maybe I was imagining it. I couldn't figure you out."

"I've been looking for you for so long."

She frowned. "You have?"

"I don't mean literally. I mean, I've been searching for someone to spend my life with. Every woman I've ever dated, or come close to dating, I've compared to you. I thought about you all of the time. Every now and then I'd try to look you up, but I never found you. And for a long time, I didn't realise that when my girlfriends didn't measure up, it was because they weren't you."

She didn't know what to think about that. They'd been so young.

"Don't get me wrong—it wasn't a romantic thing. You were just a kid, and so was I. But I was comparing them to you —their character, sense of humour, the way that you cared about other people—all things I admired in you. I held other women to that standard, and they couldn't measure up. So, when I saw you, I just wanted to be your friend. I had to spend time with you, get to know you again, because I missed you.

But then my feelings changed, and I realised I wanted more than that. I didn't know if I was completely out of line, though."

"I can understand that. I felt the same way."

"It was a big step to take. And I hated to ruin our friendship because even though we haven't known each other for long as adults, your friendship means a lot to me. I never thought I'd get the chance to see you again, and now that I have you in my life, I didn't want to mess that up."

"But the job in Boston…?"

He sighed. "I applied for that job soon after we met up that first time. I didn't know how things would go between us, and it's a great opportunity. But I realise now that you're so much more important to me than any job. If you care about me even half as much as I care about you, I'll happily turn the job down and stay here for the rest of my life. Will you give me a chance to prove my feelings for you?"

Her soul leapt. She grinned at him. "You'd turn down the job?"

"In a heartbeat."

She leaned forward to kiss him gently on the lips. "Then I guess you'd better start showing me how you feel."

"You're all I want."

They came to their feet, his arms were around her, and he pulled her into him, his lips pressed to hers. Her hands snaked around his neck, fingers wound through his hair, as his lips explored hers. Electricity coursed through her veins and her mind went blank as the two of them pressed against one another. She could see her present and her future all in one long, uninterrupted kiss.

Chapter Thirty-Four

It was never going to end. The work. It was relentless. Every step Matilda took forward, she felt as though she was pushed back two. She'd paint something, but then have to strip it again because they found mould. Or she'd fix something only to realise that there was far more broken.

She stood in the centre of the clinic and looked around. The painters weren't done, but had cancelled today. It had taken them longer than they'd thought and they had another job to go to, which left her stranded with half the work to be done and only today to finish it. She was having the new furniture delivered on Saturday and was opening for business on Monday. It didn't give her enough time. There was no way she could paint half the clinic on her own by the end of the day.

Her throat tightened, but she was determined not to cry. Tears wouldn't help, and she had to stay focused if she was going to have any chance of finishing. Just as she was about to dip her paint roller into the white paint, the front door opened, and the sound of footsteps filled her ears. Who was that?

She set the roller down, pushed the protective goggles up

onto her forehead, and stared at the entryway with her mouth agape. Ryan stood there, surrounded by his mother, father, and other family members she'd met at the BBQ. They were all dressed in work gear, most held some kind of paint brush or roller, and many wore protective goggles, hats or scarves over their hair.

Ryan grinned. "We came to help."

She ran to him and threw her arms around him, leaping into his arms at the same time. He laughed. His mother patted her on the back. The rest of the family filtered around her, calling out greetings and continuing into the building. Ryan set her feet back on the ground and got to work. She stood with her hands on her hips watching, a wide smile splitting her face in two.

She couldn't believe it. They were here. It was as though the world had been lifted from her shoulders. They could do this.

Chapter Thirty-Five

Rita put the letters down with a sigh. She'd read them all, finally. The last letter had been written by her mother, but looked as though it was never sent to Uncle Bill. It'd been hidden inside of another envelope and folded over itself until it was a tiny triangle of paper. When she unfurled it, she could see that it was a love letter, but also a goodbye. Maybe it was a draft and she sent the final version, or maybe she never told him how she truly felt. Rita would never know. She picked it up again and glanced over it.

Dearest Bill,

Even though it's been over for a while between us, that time we had together is something I'll never forget. I can't explain to you how it feels to know that I'm so well loved, and to find someone who understands and appreciates me the way you do.

But as you know, it can't go on. We both have marriages we must tend to. And even though we've been through a rough patch over these past few years, I do love your brother and I want to make our marriage work as much for the children as for myself. I hope you can understand that.

I don't think we can work together any longer now that Ray knows what happened between us. So, I won't be coming back to the café. I've already spoken with him, and he says he'll hire someone to replace me. I think it's for the best. It's your café, you shouldn't have to leave, and so, I will.

I wish you nothing but the best. I hope you know that. The time we spent together will forever be hidden in my heart. Now that the truth has come out, I'm going away for a while. I need some time to think. I can't be around Ray right now. He's so angry with me, though he says he wants to work things out. I don't know if it's possible, but I need some time away to imagine how that might go.

Take care.

Sincerely,
Sylvia

Tears blurred Rita's vision. This was a side of her mother she'd never seen. To her, Mom was lighthearted, fun, happy. She wasn't romantic or passionate. She loved Dad, but it was a convenient, casual kind of love. Nothing of the fire represented in the letter. Rita got the sense her mother was holding back, not wanting to make things any worse. There was a kind of restrained emotion behind each word.

They'd loved each other. The affair hadn't been impulsive. Or at least, not entirely. It'd gone on for months. The letter didn't say when, but perhaps years before the letter was written. When the truth was revealed somehow, her mother had gone to North Carolina to think. All of the bits and pieces of their lives made sense now. The things she'd never really understood—the tension between her parents, her father's grumpiness, the long stays in North Carolina at various times over the years... they were trying to make it work, but it was no doubt hard.

And most of all, the chasm between the two brothers. Something she'd never understood. Now it all became clear. Everyone involved was long gone—they'd passed years ago—so it was probably time to talk to Cathy about it. She and Cathy were the only people remaining who it really impacted. If it impacted them at all.

She was surprised by her own reaction to the revelations— she'd been shocked and a little sad, but it hadn't shaken her as badly as she'd imagined something like that would. She had too much drama going on in her own life to let secrets from the past shift her centre of gravity too far. But also, she'd probably always known there was something amiss. Something not quite right between her parents, and of course between the two brothers.

The office was too warm with the heat blasting. Even though the weather had finally turned cooler, she was overheating in her sweater in that small space. She got up to turn the heater down, and the door opened. Cathy stood there, two mismatched mugs held aloft.

"Tea?"

"That would be wonderful."

Cathy sat across from Rita's place at the desk. Cathy's eye makeup was particularly bright today, with a slash of yellow above the blue. Her bangs swept high over her forehead, held together with what was no doubt an impressive amount of hair spray.

Rita sighed. "I'm glad you came in. There's something I want to talk to you about."

Cathy arched an eyebrow. "What have I done now?"

"No, nothing like that. It's about the café and the past."

"Oh?"

"You know I've been reading the letters I found in that closet."

"That's right. Anything interesting turn up?"

"It did, actually. I haven't said anything before now because I wasn't sure how to raise it with you. I wanted to be able to express it in a way that you might understand, but that wouldn't cause you any pain."

Cathy set her tea down on the desk, her eyes clouding. "Now you're scaring me."

"Clearly I'm off to a great start..." Rita chuckled. "Okay, I'll just come out with it, then. My mother and your father had an affair."

"What?" Cathy's eyes widened. "No."

"Yes, it seems so. That's why Uncle Bill walked away from the café. It's why Mom, Helen and I went to North Carolina for months... do you remember that?"

"Yes, I remember. We didn't see you for ages. It felt like a lifetime."

"That's right. And it was because Dad found out about the affair."

"Oh, no." Cathy's face crumpled. "How horrible. Poor Mom."

"I don't know if she ever discovered the truth. The letters don't say. But Dad did, and he was pretty angry, apparently."

"Understandably."

"Yes, of course. So, anyway, I thought you should know. I don't have any more details. It went on for months, and Mom wrote your dad a letter expressin' her love for him, so I do think they had real feelings for each other, if that helps at all. I don't know if it does for you, but in a way it does give me some comfort."

"I suppose so," Cathy agreed. "I'm still in shock, but I guess it brings together all the pieces of our past with more clarity."

"That's exactly right. So anyway, I asked my lawyer to put together a contract that would give you half ownership of the café."

Rita waited for her words to land. It took a few seconds, but then Cathy's mouth fell open. She tried to speak a few times, but no words came out. Finally, she let out a kind of whooshing sound and then said, "Really? Rita, I don't want you to feel obligated. This is your baby."

"You've been a lifesaver these past weeks, Cathy. And I know how much you care about this place. I can't do it on my own, not anymore. I want you to be co-owner with me. We can share the responsibility and keep things going when the other can't. What do you think?"

Cathy smiled, her eyes glistening with tears. "I'd love that. Thank you, Rita. You have no idea how much this means to me."

"It's only right. Your dad was part owner of the Honeysuckle Café, and you would've inherited it except that my mother had an affair with him. And to ensure that she didn't lose her marriage, your dad gave up his dream and moved his whole family to another state. That was a big deal for all of you, and I think it's only fair that you get your inheritance back."

Rita pushed the paperwork towards Cathy and held up a pen. "All you have to do is sign, and half of this place is yours."

Tears rolled down Cathy's cheeks. She stood and came around the desk to hug Rita. They both sniffled and embraced, then sniffled some more. After a while, she sat back down, pen poised, and added her signature to the final line of the contract. They were officially business partners.

Chapter Thirty-Six

Three months later, it was Thanksgiving week, and James told Julie that he had a surprise. She couldn't imagine what it was, but they'd been dating long enough for her to realise he was a romantic and that she should be prepared for anything.

The past few months had been a whirlwind for her. Work at the café had been busy, and she'd managed to save a nice little nest egg to help her go back to school. Rita was recovering well from her treatments, and tests showed that she was finally in remission. They'd celebrated the news with a huge family gathering at the lake house that weekend. It was a party to remember. And she'd spent several nights per week with James, which was the highlight.

She had well and truly fallen for him. And the funny part was, she wasn't even a little nervous about it because he told her frequently that he felt the same way. They were falling in love, and it was a thrilling time she would never forget. She hadn't experienced anything like it before.

When he arrived to pick her up, she noticed that he wore jeans and a sweater with leather boots. So, clearly they weren't going anywhere upscale. She kissed him hello and then rushed to change into jeans as well, since her slinky dress and overcoat weren't likely to be appropriate now.

Soon, she was ready, and they headed off in his car.

"Where are we going?"

"You'll see," he replied with a smile.

Her eyes narrowed. "Come on, you have to tell me now. We're on our way there. Are we going hiking? Because it's a bit cold. Maybe bowling? Or something else... line dancing?"

He laughed. "Line dancing? You see me as a line dancer?"

She shrugged. "I don't know. You're full of secrets tonight."

"Just be patient."

"You know I can't do that."

He sighed. "It won't take long."

He was true to his word. Within fifteen minutes, he'd pulled off the main road onto a long gravelled driveway. There were oak trees lining the drive, and on either side of the trees were two grassy fields stretching into the distance and dotted with black and brown cattle.

"This is lovely," she said. "Whose place is this?"

"You can't stand it, can you?"

She folded her arms. "No, I can't. You've got to tell me— are we going to dinner at someone's house? What is this? Some kind of farm?"

"It is a farm, yes. You have amazing powers of deduction." He laughed. "But no, we're not meeting anyone for dinner."

The farmhouse was two-story, made of white timber. It looked to be at least one hundred years old, but had been reno- vated and gleamed with new paint. It was beautiful, cozy and very country. It was surrounded by a white picket fence. The driveway wound around one side of the house and stopped at a large dilapidated barn. A few chickens pecked through the dirt.

Julie breathed deeply as she stepped out of the vehicle. It was so peaceful. The air was clean and fresh. The scent of livestock lingered on the breeze. The sun was sinking down the sky and long shadows fell across the car, made her shiver and hug her arms around her sweater.

"What do you think?" he asked, coming over to lay an arm around her shoulders.

"I love it here. It's so beautiful, peaceful. It feels very homey."

"I agree."

He took her hand and led her to the house and up the stairs to the front door. Then, without knocking, he opened it and led her inside.

"What are you doing?" she objected with a laugh. "We can't just walk in, can we? Are they expecting us?"

"Who?" he asked with a wink.

She shook her head. "You've got to tell me what's going on."

In the living room, the polished timber floor gleamed. There was no furniture, other than a beautiful piano by the far window. On top of the piano sat a single lamp that threw golden light across the room. It made James' face seem to glow.

Then he got down on one knee and popped open a ring box. A platinum ring with a single diamond shone in the soft lamplight.

Julie held one hand to her mouth. Tears immediately sprang into her eyes. James reached for her other hand and held it.

"Julie, I've looked forward to this moment for as long as I can remember. I've dreamed of you, I've looked for you, and I finally found you. I don't want to spend another moment apart. You're the woman I choose for the rest of my life. Will you marry me?"

She could barely see through her tears. This wasn't what she was expecting, but she knew it was right. He was exactly the right person for her. She couldn't picture a life without him in it.

"Yes, I will marry you."

He placed the ring on her finger, then swept her up into his arms, kissing her passionately. He stepped back and she stared at the ring, unable to look away.

"It's beautiful."

"It was my grandmother's," he said. "I got it cleaned and reset for you."

"I love it. It's perfect."

"You said yes. I'm over the moon."

She grinned and kissed him again. "We're getting married."

It was growing dark in the house now, and the cold was seeping in through the open door. He led her outside again, and they sat on the porch swing out front. As they swung, with her leaning into him and his arms around her, she kept looking at her ring over and over. It sparkled with the light from the setting sun, and it fit perfectly.

"Would you like to live here after we're married?" he asked.

She sat up straight and looked into his eyes. "What? Really?"

"I hope so, because I already bought it."

She squealed with delight and kissed him again. "You really bought this place?"

"Yep. I've been looking around with a Realtor for a while, and this caught my eye. So, I bought it. There were a few people interested, and I didn't want to miss the opportunity."

"I still can't believe you turned down the Boston opportunity," she said, her brow furrowed.

He shrugged. "They commented that maybe they'd ask again in a few years and I encouraged them to do that, but for now, I'm staying put. My fiancée has a PhD to finish."

She laughed out loud and hugged him tight. "This has been the best date ever!"

Chapter Thirty-Seven

The noisy clamour of voices, barks, meows and more that came from the clinic's waiting room were music to Matilda's ears. Even after three months of operation, she couldn't get enough of it. It wasn't until the end of the first week that she realised just how much she'd missed working as a vet.

Since then, her client base had gradually picked back up to pre-renovation levels, according to the records she had in the sale documents. Everything was running well. There'd been a few hiccups with their procedures, and the first receptionist she'd inherited from the previous owner didn't work out. But they had a new receptionist now, and they were getting into a rhythm that worked for everyone.

She'd even hired another vet to work shifts with her, which had taken a load off and given her some flexibility with her schedule. She was headed home now, even though the day wasn't over. She and Ryan had a date. They hadn't done anything relaxing in forever, and they were well past due for some quality time together.

She strode out of the clinic, waving goodbye to the receptionist as the door swung shut behind her. With a smile on her face, she climbed into her car.

When she'd first learned to drive in the USA, she'd found it hard to manage the right-hand side of the road. But now, it was second nature. She still struggled occasionally at intersections, but found that following the car in front of her generally helped.

At the house, she spotted Ryan standing in the front yard, chatting over the fence with Rita. Behind Rita, Julie and her boyfriend stood hand in hand. They looked happy.

Matilda parked her car and ambled over to join them. "Hey, y'all." She loved using Southern slang. It sounded hilarious with her Aussie drawl.

They all turned to face her. Julie was beaming.

"Guess what?" Julie said, hurrying to meet her. She held up her left hand, and something bright dazzled. "We're engaged!"

Matilda grinned. "Congratulations!" She gave Julie a big hug and then stepped back to take a better look at the ring. It was dark out by now and she couldn't see it well, but it looked pretty. And she was happy for Julie. She'd been through so much in her life—it was high time something good happened to her.

Over the past few months, they'd slowly become friends. That initial conversation by the lake had led to further interactions, even a few coffees together. Matilda had begun to regard Julie as someone she could talk to about anything, or who would help her if she needed it. Julie was steadfast, kind and strong. It'd been difficult to break through into her world, but once she had, Julie had been constant in her kindness since.

Ryan shook hands with James, and then Matilda hugged him. "I'm so happy for you."

He nodded. "Thanks. I'm very happy."

Their happiness was contagious. "I've got champagne

chilling to celebrate the clinic's three-month anniversary. I'll grab it and some glasses, and we'll toast," Matilda said. "Why don't you all come upstairs to the porch, and I'll get us some food as well."

They all joined her upstairs on the porch off the kitchen overlooking the lake. Matilda turned on the outdoor heaters, and Ryan lit the outdoor fire. Then Matilda gathered glasses, champagne, and a fruit and cheese platter together while they chattered about their plans and the new farm James had bought for them to live on.

"I didn't picture you as a farm girl," Matilda said, setting everything down on the table.

Ryan poured champagne while they each grabbed a cracker with cheese or an olive.

"I've always wanted to live on a farm, to have a horse to ride and chickens to feed," Julie said, beaming at James. Then she turned to look at Matilda, her eyes glistening. "I guess he remembered."

James winked. "Of course I remembered. You've had that dream a long time. I recall you talking about it when we were kids, and I remember thinking that was a perfectly wonderful dream, and I hoped you'd get it someday. It kind of made me want to have it too. And now, here we are."

Matilda clutched her champagne flute to her chest. "You two are so romantic. I'm going to cry."

They all laughed. Then Ryan held up a glass. "To James and Julie. May they have decades of happiness together."

"To James and Julie," Rita replied with a nod.

Then they all cheered, and clinked glasses together before drinking. As the small party continued on, Ryan pulled Matilda aside to give her a welcome home kiss.

"I'm sorry I didn't get to say hello properly," he said, kissing her lightly on the nose, then the lips.

She smiled. "That's okay. Will we still have our date?"

"I think we can manage. I don't believe Rita will be up for too much of a party."

"That's true. She's looking so much better, though, isn't she?"

He nodded. "It's a relief."

"I'll get dressed in a few minutes. I need a shower, too. I had a cat pee on me today."

His nose wrinkled. "Ah, that's what that smell is."

She laughed. "You can smell it?"

"Um... I *hope* that's what I'm smelling."

"And you still hugged and kissed me. That must be love." She fluttered her eyes at him.

He dipped her and kissed her again. "It's true love."

She laughed and left to get a shower. He slapped her rear end as she walked away, and she feigned horror.

Inside the house, the phone rang. She picked it up as she walked to the bathroom. "Hello?"

"Hey, sis." The sound of Stella's voice made her smile.

"I miss you so much," she said.

"I miss you too. Just as well that I'll see you soon, then."

"You're coming to the vow renewals?" Matilda squealed.

Stella laughed. "Yep. Sean and the kids are coming too. The flights are booked. I used points for two of the tickets, which helps."

"I'm so happy. Having you there will make it all worth it."

"Well, I *am* the matron of honour, right? I can't exactly miss my baby sister's second wedding. Even if it is to her first husband. It's a very confusing thing to explain to people, by the way, but I can't wait."

"You're definitely the matron of honour. And I thought maybe I'd ask Julie to be a bridesmaid. Would that be okay?"

"That would be great," Stella said. "I think she'd love that."

"I hope so. I want to include her. I know it's been a little awkward, but I think we've moved past that."

"You're such a sweetheart," Stella said. "Oh, you know that Todd and Bryce are coming too, don't you?"

"Yes, they told me. But they're coming alone. Their families can't make it."

"It's going to be so much fun. I can't wait to see where you live and your new clinic. It all sounds amazing."

"I'm excited to show you around."

After she'd showered and dressed, she went back outside where Rita, Julia and James were all saying their goodbyes.

"I'm sorry I couldn't stick around," Matilda said. "I desperately needed to take a shower. But congratulations, you two."

"We'll see you at your wedding," Julie said, giving her a hug goodbye. "I'm looking forward to it."

"See you then."

After they'd left, Matilda and Ryan carried the food and drinks back to the kitchen.

"Where should we eat?" Ryan asked.

"Let's go to Outback Steakhouse," Matilda said with a grin. "I'm dying for a steak."

"Perfect. I'll get the Alice Springs Chicken."

"And I'll definitely need a bite or two of that," Matilda said.

Ryan grabbed her and pulled her close to kiss her on the lips. He tasted of champagne and smelled of aftershave.

"So, since you're going through with the wedding vows in front of everyone, and you've started your own business here, I guess this means you'll be staying awhile, huh?" he whispered against her hair.

"I guess it does."

"Because I'm getting used to you. You're growing on me."

"Kind of like mould?" she asked, wrinkling her nose.

He grunted. "Something like that. Only cuter."

"I think I'll stick around. There's a guy here who is totally adorable. I've got a massive crush on him."

"Who could that be?"

"It's a mystery," she said as she kissed him again.

Chapter Thirty-Eight

That week passed in a blur. There was so much to get done. Matilda had to work at the clinic, and then after work, she raced around town doing errands, finding wedding favours & decorations, getting her hair and makeup done to practice for the big day, and more.

The cake would be hummingbird, her favourite. The flowers would be pink roses, and the bridesmaid dresses were cornflower blue. Her wedding dress was stunning—she had nothing but praise for the local designer who'd pulled it together on such short notice. It was made of silk, with buttons up the back of the bodice and a low neckline. The train was semi-long, and she had a veil that almost reached the length of the dress as well. She only hoped no one stepped on it.

It was everything she'd ever wanted in a wedding and it was coming together, slowly. Ryan's mother had helped her with a lot of the details. Julie and Rita had stepped up as well, baking the cake and the desserts for the day. But Matilda had insisted on having the main course catered, since she wanted her guests to enjoy the wedding rather than spend the entire day working.

When her wedding day arrived, she woke to the sound of a car pulling into the driveway. She padded to the window with a yawn to look outside and saw a young man and woman hugging Rita. They looked like her son and daughter, who Matilda knew were both flying into town that morning. It would be good to finally meet them. Tyler Osbourne was the name that'd first brought her all the way to Covington, Georgia more than a year earlier, and there he was—standing next door. He had a buzz cut and stood like a soldier. Then he grabbed luggage from the trunk of the car and followed his mother and sister into the house.

It was time to get ready. Matilda had a shower and got dressed in white sweats. She'd chosen not to spend the night away somewhere else, since they were already married. Ryan sat up in bed, his hair a mess. He smiled at her and rubbed his eyes.

"Good morning, husband," she said.

"Good morning, wife. You ready to get remarried?"

She laughed. "I'm ready if you are."

Stella's family had gotten into town the night before and were all fast asleep in the guest room. Bryce and Todd were in the second guest room. It felt good to have a full house. Matilda made pancakes and berry compote with yoghurt for everyone, and before long, they were all up and seated around the table, eating. The children were tearing around in no time, playing with the bikes and toys Matilda had bought for them. She'd also put up a gate on the top of the stairs so they couldn't tumble down, since they were still very young, with the youngest one only recently walking.

After breakfast, Stella and Matilda went to find Julie, and the three of them set off for the hairdresser's small salon about ten minutes away. They chattered happily while they had their hair and makeup done. Then they rushed back to the house to get dressed. By now, the caterers and crew had arrived and had set up the white tent in the backyard, along with white seating and flowers. There was even a gazebo where they'd say their vows with the lake as their backdrop. It all looked incredible and made Matilda's stomach flip-flop with nervous tension.

While they got ready, a photographer flashed photos of them all together, laughing, talking, sipping champagne. It all helped to calm her nerves, and by the time she was ready to walk down the aisle, Matilda felt much better. She had nothing to be anxious about—they were already married. This part was fun.

Bryce and Todd had both agreed to walk her down the aisle. They looked at her with a mixture of pride and emotion as she met them.

"You look amazing, sis," Todd said.

Bryce bent to kiss her cheek. "You're stunning."

"Thanks," she said, smiling up at them as she linked her arms through theirs.

Within the next half hour, she and Ryan said their vows in front of fifty of their closest friends and family. It was a small group, but it was perfect. She didn't want to make it a big deal, and their yard wouldn't hold any more than that.

Then it was time to party. During the first dance, Ryan held her close and they moved as one. She let her eyes drift shut and rested her head on his chest. It felt good and safe there—she didn't want to go anywhere else, or be anyone else. Just herself, in this moment, forever.

Then she danced with Bryce, followed by Todd, and finally James.

"You'll be next down the aisle," she said to him.

He nodded. "I can't wait."

"Where will you get married?"

"I think we want to have it at the farm, but we're not in a rush. We want a summer wedding."

"Yes, it's pretty cold to have a wedding outside at this time of year. Thank goodness for my faux fur wrap," Matilda said.

"And these heaters. They're amazing."

"Aren't they?"

"I'm glad you and Julie made up."

"Me too. I think we're going to be good friends."

"She really cares about you."

"I care about her," Matilda said. "I know that I kind of blew up her life when I came here, but it blew up my life as well. Everything that happened back then hurt a lot of people, but none of it was intentional. My parents, her mother, Rita, my siblings—it's been hard on everyone, that mix-up at the surrogacy centre. But we can't turn back the clock, and we made it through."

"There's no way to deal with the past other than to accept it," James said with a nod. "I would change a few things myself, if I could. But I can't."

"Like what?"

"My parents' divorce. It was really hard on me at the time. Of course, now I can see that maybe they were better off apart. Still, I didn't get to see my dad much after that, so it really changed my life. I was angry for a long time."

"I can imagine that would've been difficult."

"But now, I'll have a family of my own. And I'm going to do everything I can to make sure it's a healthy, happy home, unlike the one where I grew up."

"I think that's a really admirable goal. I hope you guys are as happy as Ryan and I have been."

Then it was time to dance with Ryan again. Her stomach growled as he took her in his arms. "It must nearly be time to eat," she said.

"Definitely. I saw them filling up the buffet table."

"Great. I've barely eaten all day. I'm famished."

They finished the dance together. Then Ryan kissed her on the lips and led her by the hand back to their table. They sat down together. Matilda sighed. Her feet were getting sore in these heels, but she was happy. Happier than she'd ever imagined she could be.

"Are you happy?" she asked him.

He looked her in the eyes, then took both her hands and kissed them one by one. "The happiest man alive."

She stood to head to the buffet line. Ryan reached for her hand and they walked together. And Matilda glanced around at all of her family and friends gathered there. She wished her parents could've been there to see her get married. Helen and Paul too. But the blessing of their memories lingered amongst the group as everyone ate, drank, talked and laughed together. Matilda would never forget what they'd each brought into her life in their various ways and she silently thanked them for giving her such an abundance of love and family on opposite sides of the world.

THE END

WOMEN'S FICTION

THE SUNSHINE SERIES

The Sunshine Potluck Society
Four friends start a monthly potluck brunch when their lives begin to unravel.
Sunshine Reservations
An old bed and breakfast by the beach and a restaurant that was burned to the ground, give Gwen an opportunity to start afresh after divorce.
The Summer Pact
When Beth Prince was thirteen years old she met a boy on New Year's Eve at Sunshine Beach. They talked all night and when the sun rose they vowed that they'd meet back at the same place in 15 years.
A Sunshine Christmas
Maree Houston's ex-husband is back in Sunshine for

Christmas and she quickly discovers that a stolen kiss could ruin everything. Including her big secret.

CORAL ISLAND SERIES

The Island

After twenty five years of marriage and decades caring for her two children, on the evening of their vow renewal, her husband shocks her with the news that he's leaving her.

The Beach Cottage

Beatrice is speechless. It's something she never expected — a secret daughter. She and Aidan have only just renewed their romance, after decades apart, and he never mentioned a child. Did he know she existed?

The Blue Shoal Inn

Taya's inn is in trouble. Her father has built a fancy new resort in Blue Shoal and hired a handsome stranger to manage it. When the stranger offers to buy her inn and merge it with the resort, she wants to hate him but when he rescues a stray dog her feelings for him change.

Island Weddings

Charmaine moves to Coral Island and lands a job working at a local florist shop. It seems as though the entire island has caught wedding fever, with weddings planned every weekend. It's a good opportunity for her to get to know the locals, but what she doesn't expect is to be thrown into the middle of a family drama.

The Island Bookshop

Evie's book club friends are the people in the world she relies on most. But when one of the newer members finds herself confronted with her past, the rest of the club will do what they can to help, endangering the existence of the bookshop without realising it.

An Island Reunion

It's been thirty five years since the friends graduated from Coral Island State Primary School and the class is returning to the island to celebrate.

THE WARATAH INN SERIES

The Waratah Inn
Wrested back to Cabarita Beach by her grandmother's sudden death, Kate Summer discovers a mystery buried in the past that changes everything.

One Summer in Italy
Reeda leaves the Waratah Inn and returns to Sydney, her husband, and her thriving interior design business, only to find her marriage in tatters. She's lost sight of what she wants in life and can't recognise the person she's become.

The Summer Sisters
Set against the golden sands and crystal clear waters of Cabarita Beach three sisters inherit an inn and discover a mystery about their grandmother's past that changes everything they thought they knew about their family...

Christmas at The Waratah Inn
Liz Cranwell is divorced and alone at Christmas. When her friends convince her to holiday at The Waratah Inn, she's dreading her first Christmas on her own. Instead she discovers that strangers can be the balm to heal the wounds of a lonely heart in this heartwarming Christmas story.

EMERALD COVE SERIES

Cottage on Oceanview Lane
When a renowned book editor returns to her roots, she rediscovers her strength & her passion in this heartwarming novel.

Seaside Manor Bed & Breakfast

The Seaside Manor Bed and Breakfast has been an institution in Emerald Cove for as long as anyone can remember. But things are changing and Diana is nervous about what the future might hold for her and her husband, not to mention the historic business.

Bungalow on Pelican Way

Moving to the Cove gave Rebecca De Vries a place to hide from her abusive ex. Now that he's in jail, she can get back to living her life as a police officer in her adopted hometown working alongside her intractable but very attractive boss, Franklin.

Chalet on Cliffside Drive

At forty-four years of age, Ben Silver thought he'd never find love. When he moves to Emerald Cove, he does it to support his birth mother, Diana, after her husband's sudden death. But then he meets Vicky.

An Emerald Cove Christmas

The Flannigan family has been through a lot together. They've grown and changed over the years and now have a blended and extended family that doesn't always see eye to eye. But this Christmas they'll learn that love can overcome all of the pain and differences of the past in this inspiring Christmas tale.

MYSTERIES

White Picket Lies

Fighting the demons of her past Toni finds herself in the midst of a second marriage breakdown at forty seven years of age. She struggles to keep depression at bay while doing her best to raise a wayward teenaged son and uncover the identity of the killer.

In this small town investigation, it's only a matter of time until friends and neighbours turn on each other.

About the Author

Lilly Mirren is an Amazon top 20, Audible top 15 and *USA Today* Bestselling author who has sold over two million copies of her books worldwide. She lives in Brisbane, Australia with her husband and three children.

Her books combine heartwarming storylines with realistic characters readers see as friends.

Her debut series, *The Waratah Inn*, set in the delightful Cabarita Beach, hit the *USA Today* Bestseller list and since then, has touched the hearts of hundreds of thousands of readers across the globe.